Raw

Jennifer Kilgore-Caradec

Raw

LE LYS BLEU
ÉDITIONS

ISBN : 979-10-422-0095-4

For Christy
and for Zelda
all ways
always

The illustrations of this volume were created and/or photographed by the author.

"Pep Talking the Alphabet" was first published in homage to Dr. Denis Mukwege *Lisa e-journal* (2020). "Aunt Eileen" was first published as "Eileen's Polluted Waterways Tours" in the online journal *Academic Exchange* (2005). "The Cattle Are Lowin': A Postcard from Michigan" was first published in *Cahiers de la MRSH* 36 (2004).

Thanks for suggestions concerning aspects of the manuscript to Ron Smith, Angelika Schober, and Chantal Fouquet.

How to

La vie n'est supportable que si l'on y introduit non pas de l'utopie mais de la poésie, c'est-à-dire de l'intensité, de la fête, de la joie, de la communion, du bonheur et de l'amour.

Edgar Morin, *Vers l'abîme (2007)*

To sacrifice something is to make it holy by giving it away for love.

Frederick Buechner, *Beyond Words (2004)*

Il y a des êtres qui justifient le monde, qui aident à vivre par leur seule présence.

Albert Camus, *Le Premier Homme (1994)*

I

(Market Day, Stand 2)

Get your shortest
poems here —
2 for the price of one:
Get Pound's "In
a Station of the Metro"
with or *without*
its original
punctuation

(Mind the gap/s
and gas/p
at the phallic
symbol? yeah!
you too, Nancy?).

II

Like an envelope that opens
closes
opens
Emily D's obsession
with Sue

Or how to make
love
with
words

III

Jane and Joan
were quite well known

Jane (aka Geneviève) saved Paris
from Attila, getting wheat to eat

and Joan, well everybody knows her story —
eat barbecue, she would not do

IV

Amanda Gorman, yes
their Rapture-Rupture at the Capitol, no
but yes, we will always remember
Officers Jones and Goodman
fighting hand-to-hand combat
and senators crouching under seats
trying to find gas-masks —
without *them*, no USA in 2026
for the 250th

V

Target practice, why?
Try learning to compost and grow vegetables

People were dropping like flies with virus
while he lied, while he lied, while he lied

VI

Early positive / bonds help kids cope with trauma: / regulation skills.

Some schools offer a / support system in classrooms. / Kids may need treatment.

Strategy to use: / reassurance, and routine. / Add regulation.

Don't expect to be / perfect: who is? Parents should / be kind to themselves.

Figs stuffed with goat-cheese: / the appetizer you need / to get through this now.

Cut each fig in half / lengthwise. Press with spoon. Mash cheese / in. Drop almonds on.

Or in camper-van / get blue cheese, cream cheese, and mix, / form into a ball,

chill for an hour, / cover with hazelnuts, and / serve with bread and wine.

VII

« Avec toi je veux partir toute la vie
sur les routes du monde entier »

[…]

« marcher dans l'inquiétude et l'incompréhension
au lieu des certitudes de bonne réputation »

— Jeanine Deckers

VIII

Bye 2020! / Blursdays are gone, we hope, in / 2021.
In Hawaii, the / word for salt is pa-akal, / solidify sea.
Solidify me / to cope with damned covid time / and keep nurses safe.

IX

How to survive
"A city built upon mud;
A culture built upon profit"

MacNeice understood.
Stand and Sing
Your Own Songs.
Own Your Songs.

X

It’s the planet —
We’re all
immigrants
vortexing
here —
in this
climate
in this
anthropocene
weather

XI

Pour tes beaux yeux qui me font revivre,
(si rare ces goûts qui coïncident)

Cœur de Rose,
garde un petit pétale pour moi

XII

A M O R
M   O
O   M
R O M A

To Michigan

When you are stalked you never know what is at stake:
though the governor of the Great Lakes State
did not lose her life in the middle of a lake.

It's Thanksgiving in Michigan of the blue and watery hues.
During and after the journey, covid's reality looms—
Some gather, some are alone, some sing the blues.

But do newspapers print a few poems? once thought Guest:
"We've come for a time to be just what we are.
Here we can talk of ourselves and be frank."

It's true, some people still sing Rodriguez songs.
And, Michiganders deserve a poet laureate too—
Be it a day for Will Carleton or not.

Some of his lines still ring rather true:
"For her eyes my eyes enlisted more than books on any shelf,
And no lesson e'er existed so instructive as herself."

But by 1916 he was already a has-been
receiving only a passing scoff on
page 327 of September's *Poetry*

that printed poems by Ezra P and a certain
"Mr. T. R. Eliot, an American poet resident abroad"
[sic], who probably never once visited Michigan

or heard of Carleton day, October 21.
But they must have known of the first
Poet Laureate of Michigan in the 1950s

After which, nothing, no-one in their prime…
unless it be Philip Levine, Robert Hayden,
Theodore Roethke, Carolyn Forché or Tyehimba Jess…

(Some were published by Harriet Monroe)
Or the ones that taught a while at U of M or K or MSU,
like Donald Hall, Conrad Hilberry, Janine Certo, or Diane Seuss?

Who is a Michigan poet? Would Carl Sandburg
fit, for writing so well about Lake Michigan water? Or Ishmael
Reed, for winning an award in the state?

Only one of five states to have no poet laureate
for over sixty years! A whole lifetime…. Still,
my mother loved Gwen Frostic and taught me to, too.

Flint (and its water) landed its first poet
laureate in 2019 — and Semaj Brown got
50,000 dollars to get children to poetry.

At last, in 2023, Michigan was like Sleeping Beauty:
Nandi Comer take a bow — but be careful
in which ring (just joking)! You are

in the fight for poetry, where all languages
and communities, even Detroit, fit.
Langston Hughes would have loved it!

Bingo 2020

January was a good month, a fresh start,
a new calendar, new pen and paper

February was routine with a rumor
pregnant with hidden truths of far-off menace

March marched in military-propaganda-style
with war discourse, control and curfew in China and Europe

April saw the dead pile up in New York
How many more everyone wondered

May was beautiful but the joy of spring was
missing after George Floyd's murder

June was not a new tune when the virus hatred
blues intensified in Michigan, Mississippi, and Minnesota

July we tried to imagine we could have
vacation as usual, but it wasn't

August of Bielorussia elections, explosion in Beirut, Putin poison,
refugees of California fires, flooding in Louisiana and the Caribbean

September we needed some rest finally, not back-to-school
as planned, with masked(?) students or on ventilators

October was the month everyone fell ill
and schools were prone to go remote

November all at home we could watch the elections
and the denial of their real results

that carried on into December and right up to
January 6, 2021, Humpty-Dumpty

My Momma I asked

Her birthday was a flag waver
to the moon and back
Momma always cried singing
the national anthem

said it made her think of the war
born in '39, a rough time
her childhood seemed
and busy, busy with moving

school to school, rule to rule,
two fathers, two mothers,
a couple of aunts filling in
evenings and weekends

and grandparents on that farm
(that's why the arboretum)
skirt up one week, down the next
mother's length, grandmother's length

negotiating not easy, but for
a child hardly noticeable
and that day they walked together
home from school, just talking

no way can you date a young
black man, my dear, that just
cannot happen here—unanimous they said:
that will be over right now

and some years later
they all moved to the suburbs
white flight, you know, 1967
was a rough year for shopkeepers

that man tied to a chair in the basement
when the building caught fire
or that doctor whose office nobody
touched, cause he always took them in

they could be polite, those others,
the pronoun Oates found out all about
and that Brooks took it on herself
for commemorative purposes

Momma was torn by it, I tell you
she may have even seen it coming
BLACK LIVES MATTER
to be seen from the moon

and back on the anniversary of her death
D-Day, sure was eh? anyone
notice there were no Americans
in Normandy this year?

They had the cemetery covered
though, the Normans wanted to fill
in for the memorial detail, and
some tricolor jets flew over

and back to the beginning
when I asked my Momma
why she jumped when that man
was standing at the screen door

Oh honey, I just hadn't noticed him
and was afraid. I understand
Momma, since then I've been afraid many times
to figure out how that fear was built into us.

Pep Talking the Alphabet

Apples are a fruit
a way of ending a meal
a snack you can grow at home
a gift on a tree
a home to a worm
a taste burst of variety and color—
cultivating taste and flavor
(think wine, think tea, think *liqueur,* think chocolate—
and especially: think with all five senses)
a portable lifter of spirits
A gift from Eve to Adam
A howl of adorable and after
and all eternal nows

Better you can always be
better than bullies bullying bull
or a best be campaign that is not even grammatical
but before you think it's all about
bug-out bags ready
buster beaches maybe it's not about politics
but about recreation breaks at school or
brute internet trollers
Batter batter batter SWING—
B has always been a better letter than that.

Gatsby — Read J. Gatz BE.
B—I—N—G—O—! Saul Bellow told you so.
Ben Franklin took his penny to Auray.
Is your Armorican Dream better than mine?

C is homonym of command, see—
(Cult-Culture-Cultivation with Creativity)
that, like B, can be a verb in shorthand,
on your cell phone, mobile device, portable computer
C has come of age with AI. The great C of shining seas
catapulting computing to highways of—tune in, Renée—

Capitalism Capitalism Capitalism Capitalism

Charge on now! only to discover that
Change is a way of life
cliché clichéd Covid cliché
collapse and/or die chaos
but champions do not need much
compensation (crashed with the economy)
come chivalry season
Crane(d) both Stephen and Hart.
C vitamins. Smart people C
And now for some collapsology.
Clap—Clap—Clap

Damn it! I'll be damned!
Damnèd! in French — an expression to get you around that
damn corner of words in C like Covid Crash
Die after you've survived *Danse Macabre*?
Doctors and Nurses, and all hospital personnel, we thank you.
Did your last public outing commemorating
Pastor Michel Leplay who

did never before distance socially
around dozens of people, with music.
Then went into LockDown / Confinement / The Damned Time
(this letter D is not approved for children)
Life is Beautiful! with devastation in D-Minor
Did all those cashier ladies at the supermarket just disappear?
Damnèd—pardon my French.
The Beautiful and the Damned
Democracy shut-down and Hertz hurts
(Diderot, where'd his University go?)
Doers and riskers, cleaners and garbage-collectors we thank you.
Undertakers we thank you. Refrigerator truck-operators
we thank you.
People who cut animals for us to eat, we thank you.
Don't they bury the dead any more? Funerals for Five?
Damn waiting in line to go inside supermarkets.
Damn not finding what you want when inside.
Grocery delivery truck drivers we thank you.
Drink quarantinis? Darn your socks?
Damn first world problems. Listen to Dizzy Gillespie?
Dive into the trash for food?
Drive yourself crazy? or DIY and some Distractions?
Do get your exercise.
Damn them! think the leaders: too much free time
They'd rise up and we'd be toppled. Let's damn that right there.
Do all of you go back to work right now. Die if you must.

Earth Day — just in time,
easy-going Ruth's birthday and
Eileen, like Jane Goodall,
approves of Greta Thunberg,
Eke out your living
Earth, to the moon and back we love you.

We love you, we promise we do.
Earth our mother, Gaia (see the letter G),
Thank you for existing in us.
Thank you for being so eccentrically beautiful
with bursts of color and pizzazz of eclectic dazzle
and creaturely inventiveness of sense and senses
sounds and curves, rounds, spots,
tastes, squares, smells and spittle.
Eagerly, though without a camera,
Emily Dickinson caught that bird hopping—for forever.
Your creatures are us, and we are they, like them
though sometimes we think we think more
than others, animals and plants,
Earth of soil and spoil, we still live and toil
and *I love Paris in the Springtime*
ecstatically excellent bird-filled springtime
defying T.S. Eliot's April
Hear ye Hear ye! all Americans are
Equal under the law.
Excellent, those photos by Dale Vanderheyden!
Ever wished I were a bird, crazy to make lists
i.e. Alcatraz Atlántico, Sula bassana, Havssula, Jan-van-gent,
Fous de Bassan
Either you let your neighbour know before you leave or—
Enter etiquette and being neighborly on the Île Rouzic—
where everyone has a place.

Fuck having 300,000 deaths by mid-May
        You heard that right brothers and sisters,
        and so many more on the way
Fuck having the equivalent of 10,000 airplanes crash
        around the world in less than three months:
That's more than 30 planes crashing every damn day!

Fuck not seeing and hearing the mourners,
Fuck not seeing the dying die
Fuck not seeing their names written in a line running from here to
Mars with Elon's funk
Fuck *For your information, we do need to keep morale up*
Fuck *so you do not just go into free-fall or*
Fuck *throw in the towel, or commit suicide*
Fuck *like those university students stuck in their dorm rooms*
Fuck *with no money, no food, and no hope*
Fuck there being no vaccine yet, or maybe ever
Fuck having truth be the first casualty of war and
Fuck this thing being called a war and
Fuck not hugging you anymore

Garden it out of you, the anger and the hunger
Garden therapy in your small room in
London, New York, Paris, Rome, Shanghai,
Tokyo, Berlin, Moscow, the Cruise Ship, Mumbai.
Grow lettuce from seeds in two weeks.
Great! Radish seeds sprout in seven days.
Glover's clover or just stand up and
Garden for Gaia or Grandma (are they so different?).
Grab all you need to know on YouTube—or call her,
she'll tell you—
six hours a day of sunlight is enough, or
get light fixtures.
Graft your beans and fruit trees.
Garden-for-Life during Apocalypse, you have the right to
Get thee to thy gym in one square meter.
Get mental health checks in your tiny space on-line.
Read Jorie Graham. Have you still got running water? Is it
safe to drink?
Gurus and Google, if Granny's gone,
will carry you through. Meditation?

G-Train on the weekend and *Peace Train* and
Garfunkel and Simon would never eat a *guga*—
No Guns for sale, and, as always *How Green was My Valley*
the Great Outdoors will still be there someday, if you will be.

Heather Heyer may be reading there too.
Hats off right here to Tony Harrison and Geoffrey Hill
If anything can get us through this, poets will.
Not that this piece demonstrates a poet's skill
But feel free to read all poets whose names begin with H—
They'll take you to one hankering place
Where superlatives will be on hold, and
That word (huge) has been banished forever.
"Faire words butter noe parsnips" yet
some perform better than others, see
Speech! Speech!

Information Society
You use internet? Internet use you?
You use internet? Internet use you?
Algorithm algorithm campus campus campus
algorithm algorithm campus campus campus
algorithm algorithm youtube youtube youtube
algorithm algorithm youtube youtube youtube
algorithm algorithm facebook facebook facebook
algorithm algorithm facebook facebook facebook
algorithm algorithm amazon amazon
algorithm algorithm tiktok tiktok tiktok
algorithm algorithm reddit reddit reddit
algorithm algorithm instagram instagram
algorithm algorithm google google google
algorithm algorithm baidu baidu baidu

algorithm algorithm alibaba alibaba
algorithm algorithm medium medium
algorithm algorithm wechat wechat wechat
algorithm algorithm weibo weibo weibo
algorithm algorithm twitter twitter twitter
algorithm algorithm twitter twitter twitter
algorithm algorithm bing bing bing bing bing
algorithm algorithm snapchat snapchat snapchat
algorithm algorithm bitters bitters bitters
I spy—let's play!—I spy I spy I spy I spy I—
AI AI AI AI AI AI AI
data campus data campus data campus data data
data campus data campus data data data
you use internet / internet use you
you use internet, internet use you.

Just where are you planning to go to escape that
Juggernaut? jug-jug-jug, so rudely forced
decades of being weaned from books
replaced by screams from screens.
Screens to keep out the heat and the insects are
just what you need. Ratch it up, a few more
notches up in summer and it
just won't be viable to live here any more.
joy-ride under-the-water, in-the-heat,
over-the-desert, into-the-election
jingoism-storm. Just let us sp-p-p-pray.
Jojoba grows in the US, and *is* American English.
Jokeless joker jollifying jolts to Joseph and Mary.
Johnny get your gun and take it to school. Jotty the joss house.
Just jazzing their white supremacy jabberwoky. Enjoy.
Jonah, where are you? Our joules are solar, or should be.
Jenner and Pasteur set a precedent: free vaccines.
Journalists and journalism need our support.

Keep calm and carry on—are you kidding?
The nation is dyeing itself pure white
and we don't know the real death count in kakotopia.
Kalamatas we are nibbling as we watch
kakistocracy on the news.
The kakkerlaks have come out of the woodwork.
Kangeroos and Koalas went in the fires.
Koans were given for cornucopias.
Klannishness is in (out-of-a-fashion).
Ka-Ching! How many golden eggs until the goose stops cackling?
Krag-Jørgensen anyone?
It gives me the creeps.
Kendall uses a kindle?
Kraak-porselein is my preference, truth be told.

Leading is never easy, but now
our leaders are trying, and some might be wishing
to try something else for a while
learn all you need to know
about leading from these leaders of now
learn about elections
Lead to elect or be elected
Be elected to lead
Leaning right, leaning left;
lean in towards the truth—
don't betray your youth or our youth.
Our Last Dance with Democracy is all about the—
50,000,000 that died, an estimation, (at the end
and just after World War I)
"Candy is dandy but
liquor is quicker"
than your composting adventures
(that was a word from our sponsor)—

Infinity box—mind the gap!
83 million population count in Germany
8,428 dead by end May 2020.
Dr. Seuss died before your time.
Leave you to read *Into the Forest.*
All I wanna do is have some Phoenicia,
not garden Grandma.

Money Charles Péguy did not like
Misery was worse; avoid misery at all cost, but
Meatless Mondays might have pleased him.
Mask-less would he have been this May?
Me thinks not, and even less manipulated.
Mask for what? He did not live long enough
to get the mustard—after getting the bullet
smack in the forehead he was gone pretty fast.
Still muddy, some of his generation lived through 1914-1918
only to die of the flu. Most likely never understood that
until now. Thought so many worn out after war,
minus those in the Necropole Nationale de Chambry,
but epidemics can kill gore galore—
minus three percent of world's population—
virus that killed Apollinaire. Where were those
many buried? Undertakers were and are
overwhelmed. Where were morticians
in Faulkner's *As I lay dying?* No money for the
morgue, so make your own coffin or
be buried in a cardboard box on NYC's Hart Island or
mass grave in a Pennsylvania
meadow uncovered in 2015.
Miracles happen: mass graves can be sold
// and erosion will erode //
Mention it—more than 670,000 dead in the United States then—

(might as well admit no one thinks it started in Spain).
Memorial Day this year: 100,000 or near—
Some here some there, death is catching everywhere
tsunami of 2004 maybe 225,000, just after more heat,
—more—summer 2003: almost 20,000 in France
and 20,000 in Italy.
Memorize New Orleans August Two Thousand O Five,
Morus Bassanus,
meeting NYC—which hurricane was it—Sandy?
only 285 died, but it flooded the MTA with bills, so
make believe lower Manhattan can cover
540 vulnerable openings in a
mere six subway stations with sandbags
every time another one comes round?
m-m-m-m-m-m-my ass not covered!
meteorologists registered 40° Celsius
merely—in Lille—and 43.6° (104 and 110°F) in Saint-Maur-des
Fossés (Val-de-Marne) in 2019 and 1,500 melted (euphemism).
Mascara still on?—December 11, 1960—
la liberté ne se donne pas
mais s'arrache, oh *Algérie Mon Amour*
—Tree pods and memory forests—seriously? in floods or deserts?
More—order more—DIY gravesites, as Steinbeck
marked it and prayed it in *Grapes of Wrath.*
Low estimates: 17.5 million in WW1, 56.4 million in WW2—
Mention that here? *The Shock Doctrine* observed by Naomi Klein
missed not the playbook after Twin Towers
were trumped. Lovely boy
must have been two then, but is still afraid of flying.
Meanwhile infrastructures' mileage is worn
pretty thin: Genoa's bridge,
Midland in Michigan, just more water over the dam
making kids sick in Flint. *Sous le pont*
Mirabeau coule la Seine… Mont Saint-Michel?—been there,

done that.
Muddy Waters sang *Manish Boy* and *She's Nineteen Years Old*
My Oh My! Negro spiritual, Soul and
prosperity gospel do not mix.
MacNeice never so confused, but "Mayday" was
all Muldoon could muster.
Miffed, she asked, Is Democracy dead already?

Now what? Now you are graduating—oh my God—in May 2020?
No ceremony, no cap and gown,
No pictures with Mom and Dad in a crowd.
No pomp and circumstance,
No graduation party.
Not even a moment's notice, then negations
Of everything you thought would be—
Not *Que sera sera* with Doris Day singing so sweetly
in that movie—
Not to bereave you of any comfort at all,
No, lucidity is its own gift
Northern Gannet.
Now people are forced to think about their lives,
Nesting in place, sift and identify the essential
Negotiate the knuckled and the known, thinking of
Freedoms overthrown, the needs of now, but
Newness will come sooner or later
Newness for you with all sweetness,
Neighborly being, rise to meet the sweetness.
Now you can begin making it right where you are.

O say can you see a way through or sing in the key of C?
Ogden Nash can make anyone like poetry
Or is that only rhyming or advertising written wryly?
O say, C major or C minor?
Oy, out with praise and lament

Oe already knows poetry can make anything happen,
on and on those nursery rhymes
Of Man's first disobedience, and the fruition of Margaret Atwood.
Oyster-like would be better? Oates, Joyce Carol
Oximeters are efficacious it seems—
oolong tea also works in a pinch; breathe in steam
(slowly) breathe out (ahhh) —or with peppered curcuma—
breathe in iambic pentameter? can you?
How much do you let out when you speak
out at, say, commencement? Obama's fault, oh?
One generation passes away, another generation comes,
but the earth remains forever.

Pretty please
My pet, my poet, my prop,
let us propel ourselves
into the future, my
pop corn and your prayers,
putting our pettiness aside
to prosper differently
propitiously—
Oh Pangolin,
what is prosperity
if not prepping
for the unprepared—
pill jars and pineapples
out with the pork roast
in with the primavera vegetarian pizza
—pinch the pretty pink-tongued kitty—
instead it's time for purple potatoes
Pommes Pont-Neuf
with pulses and pickles,
pasta with pesto,

polenta and peppers, my pomegranate,
anything in your pantry,
pound for pound,
poverty be damned.

Quoheleth quacked that he knew more—while
quota rationed rationing quorum
quoad hoc sex offences and
quite a number of quids for DSK since registering on Guernesey
quoth Quixote quickly, last time they met.
Quiller-Couch of course they were not reading
Quit then, not reading this either. Your
quilting grandma heard the Queen's speech and
quoted back: unity bracelets on, brace up.

Resurrect Resilience and
Bring back bicycles and picnics in bike baskets
over a checkered red-and-white tablecloth on the grass.
Romaine lettuce standing up to Repression
Roma-Amor Delores and Ron Smith
Repeat the nurses had no P.P.E. Repeat
Record it: they told the people not to wear face masks
Rear-up to the Rubicon, why not tell them:
make your own masks?
surely not because Macronism's rote is that
the poor should not do more
Enough is enough or Hénaff is Hénaff?
Resistance and Right-of-way
Rights of passage and right to die at home,
Right to be rich, richer, richer, richer, richer (ad infinitum)
Right to die without a ventilator
RE. my covid body strapped above TGV seats on the Paris-Brest

Reserved for medical purposes the ticket reads
Real life is full of such conundrums between life and death
Oh, is it *Laudate Si* Week?

Say it, play it, sing it if you can:
"A bird doesn't sing
because it has an answer it sings
because it has a song"— said Maya Angelou.
sparrows are back in Paris —
how many years had I not seen them?
Sing for Your Supper
Sing about something else and do
(Shit! Fuck! Damn! was often said
sometimes to the kakoprick spilling sluff on TV)
sing in complete sentences about
seeing the Notre Dame fire from your apartment window and
seeing it on TV simultaneously.
So sing about Lassana Bathily, and those who
sufferered tragedy at Charlie Hebdo and Bataclan,
sorrow upon sorrow. And ashes all the way to
Seeing Things, that symposium so aptly timed to
some terrorists' calendars, but still we visited the
Château de Chenonceau.
Shall we yet save the alphabet?
Sing about the English language from
Shakespeare to Ashbery, letter by letter it
stands or falls, the meaning is in the details, and time
(thank you Monique, thank you Marcelle)
stands still for actions that speak louder than words,
sly in the humour and the slant,
say teachers *do* (a performative verb, thank you),
and those who can't
should do something different—

How many sirens a day?
slang sometimes speaks even louder—
slung posters over roundabouts more in-
spired than spraying graffiti at the tomb on the
Champs-Élysées—only a young dead body—
some no-one-from-nowhere in there after all—
Spitals then even worse than now?
Sula Sgeir as Peter May told it
Surefire starting point come San Jordi.
People to power: power to People
say what? Jefferson's library did
not keep him from *having* slaves?
Say you missed the 100,000?
SC, NC, and MD had that many in 1790,
Shy of 300,000 in Virginia back then
Statues came down, but still—
NYT's front page on May 24, 2020.

Tea, I drink with jam and bread
Today is the first day of the rest of your life
Triteness identified is not poetry
Too much cliché, too little pizzazz
Too much pizza too little those jeans
Too long a shutdown and pop goes the weasel
(it's the economy, stupid).
To be or not to be made in France
The Made in France salon as a concept store
Tourism destination #1. *Bird by bird.*
Teachers need a raise too.

Upper classes are something you need to be born into or go
on to other things, like education and opportunity
unusual to get ahead there, unless you're already ahead and
use the dictionary, unless you are playing scrabble, and
up that hill difficulty, as they say, angry young person,

unless you get lucky, you won't rise far but it's all
up to you, that's what they need you to know,
useless is your struggle, because you did not have it in you to
upgrade your game or your name. You know you are not good
enough, don't you? University education taught you that, didn't it?
up is down, down is up, it's a perspective.
underdeveloped, like countries, through no will of their own
up yours catch-up culture catch-up ketchup
until how old, how far—and what that means!—
until Every Man a King!
(https://www.youtube.com/watch?v=nfu_pLb0swA)

Versailles was that golden age where
The upper classes hung out together
Very glamorously in the King's gardens
Manière de montrer les jardins de Versailles
With the water music and the fountains
And the well-trimmed pathways, though
Today one might think not enough gold toilets
But the gardens are fab—all round internet access
—Lully-Rameau-the French Opera-and leading to Haendel—
Good thing too, how could you get along without?
Richelieu aimait *le chocolat à boire*, as did Mazarin,
How hot was chocolate long before it came to Versailles?
"*La Reine n'a que deux passions: le roi et le chocolat*"
"The profit of the earth is for all: the king himself is
Served by the field" (Quoheleth)
And the king himself was a gardener, along with Le Nôtre, and so
The Kings Treasures of Literature and
Oranges and lemons from Spain,
Italy, and Portugal. Lovingly Louis
Le Vau arranged their walls and windows for the largest
European indoor orange groves. So tell me, whatever happened to

Michele Obama's White House Kitchen Garden,
Or your grandmother's rose garden, or
Kew Gardens and their seed banks, prospering since 1759?
Every nation, every inner city, every suburb, has its high points,
—My King, Martin Luther—
Where culture overflows the Versailles fountains or
That bouquet vase
(there are other kings around: Roy Haynes,
Leroy Jones, B.B. King)
All the King's Men
So long as there is little vexation of spirit, just so—
Very Seralini—at the flooded Svalbard Seed Vault
Vamp it up, vamoose vice and violence and patented pickles, all
Vittles are yours—remember Vatel, who died
From an overdose of Chantilly, as in stress and burn-out, but
Valediction to your DIY seed gathering exchanges
Vet that and the Vetch President does too—Dekalb and
DeVos be damned.

Women were first employed in the factories
and "dark Satanic Mills"
—William Blake's *Jerusalem* coined it—
and later as gardeners at Kew in 1896.
Who are you woman?
Why do you want to be president?
Being the president's wife was not rewarding?
Re-ward her right away.
Stay-at-home moms educate their children at home.
A time to rend, and a time to sew
Was that written wryly? A time to
Weep and a time to laugh
What if Harvard, Yale, Princeton or Purdue
Whittled down their names every 3 or 4 years?

Wherefore I praised the dead
which are already dead
more than the living which are yet alive.
Resurrect resilience, but not for work.
WFH looks so much like WTF
where is home now? Hong Kong? Shanghai?
Two are better than one… and how can one be warm alone?
Wainwright is the poet, not me—but I can make face masks
When will it happen? When? Mask on paper
something to die for? cf.
Williams, *Descent into Hell*
without water how will they wash their hands?
A time to keep silence, and a time to speak—

Xylophones and zephyrs
on the way from alpha to omega
via old McDonald's poetry farm
xylocopids, xiphoids, and President Xi
and the impeachment trials reruns
xanthine, more xanthine?
droning on and on
over those deserted-looking cities
I only am escaped alone to tell thee
one rule, two measures: choose
e.e. cummings or Dominic Cummings
X factor for 5G and Arthur Firstenberg?

YouTube's algorithms gave us
binge-watch usage of conspiracy theories and
your virus is my virus. Take it down Facebook!
How did *that* spread so fast?
Help me leave my screen and get back to

the books on my shelves or
Yankee doodle went to town… (read all about it!
Y'all know that song went viral)
You, time with you, an evening together with
candlelight, reading Yeats or *Yentl*
You've been here before.
Yseult and Tristan, she loved them. Héloïse and Abélard,
I miss her.
Yves, Saint-Yves, priez-pour-nous (who knew she loved Yves
Saint Laurent?)
Yo, the Latin alphabet, even our English, will survive
yonder after we all speak 中文, if we do
you know, and if we don't—superlative!
yon one percent yawn, and yet!
Yes-women are over—see Christine Blasey Ford
yielding herself to months of hell to prove it
(polygraphed August 7),
yes Corey Booker said it best: "the culture of our country"—
your land is my land, with increased pro-bono legal council.

Zelda's guys were all keen to play trumpet and stuff
but they texted to say they couldn't make it—
Zarzuela keeping them busy.
Wanna share a poppy-seed bagel? a bloody Mary?
Zippy celebration's gonna be just us.
Zoom me at 6? code: Kalamazoo-zoo-zoo-zoo-zoo-zoom
you see the penguins in lockdown?
Zoo in Lincoln Park is the best
Zola last week? Plato's *Republic* next, and the
Zohar's fine reading for a windy night.
Better is a poor and wise child than an old and
foolish king, who will no more be admonished.
Joyce was a Zuricher by the end. Was he or

wasn't he a Catholic writer? Only his hair-dresser knows if
zig-zagging cats count—"Mkgnao!"—C°a°t°h°o°l°i°c frolic
Zugzwang *Finnigan's Wake.* Another
Zogist died yesterday.
Zomboids just don't get it—
zone the bastards?
Get some *ZZzzZZzzZZzz…*
ZIP code episode of UNTIED States with NO
quash-the-vote postal service
Zero mercy in their minds
Zilch—and they are armed to the teeth. The
Zou-Zou are dying fast—zounds!
ZPG whose objective? call it
zufolo rice krispie cracker jack quartet?
Crown by Chikka or Stormzy instead and
Zap the Futures Industry Association
Zowie there are zillions and
other ways and means committees
with less
zeal and more love
le Ménez hom, la Pointe du Raz
the Appalachia and the Ozarks,
zibib ouzo ozone—sing
Zamen! Amen O Mega
Z

(April-mid May 2020)

Into the Forest

We were walking
maybe only five or ten minutes
away from concrete
around an artificially produced
lake with some real

trees and shrubs
a few fish and ducks
but no one fishing
at that moment
of the afternoon

the water was gleaming
glimpsed through new
tenderly trembling leaves
in the brisk sunlight
turning on the path
toward the water
she was facing the wind and
pulled out a colorful scarf that fluttered
and caught my eye sparkling
as she drew it slowly around her neck
and suddenly transformed
into a tingling *sylphide* in
silky dazzling flowers

the magic was brief and sharp
my breathing paused—
but I had no idea
how deeply it cut

As Victor Hugo said to
Sylphide, the ballerina,
À vos pieds, à vos ailes.

(2022)

Meanwhile

Meanwhile families were being torn against each other
in Aleppo the bombing raged, the tanks rumbled
and children and women were shredded in
their basement hiding spots,
still clutching their toys. But they did not
show that on TV.

On the 13th of December Aleppo fell.
And fell. And then a walking
hell of lines of people trying to escape
bombs and bullets.

Meanwhile all the media seemed caught
in the continued roil of American elections
with social media swirling, just like
the cancerous election maps of the USA.

Meanwhile, families were divided
Staccato warning messages and threats
exchanged with sparks.
Can the tone come down a notch?

We can no longer eat in front of the news.
They are killing doctors in retaliation.

(2016)

Is that the right question?

It’s less likely you’ll meet
sexual aggression
in the Trans Bathroom than
at the doctor’s office
in the department store
or at the beauty pageant
(where we know how
he grabbed them
—he told us so).

Forced sex with your sports coach or
in the university, in the professor’s office
or in the confessional
or with the gynaecologist, while you are strapped in,
or with your uncle or your father or your grandfather,
or by the barbarous king so rudely forced,
(Rum place for a cigar, Herr Präsident)
happens, more than we care to know.

No grown woman has ever said
they never encountered
inappropriate behavior from men
while on public transport, walking down
the street, or reading on a park bench.
Or when they asked for a raise or promotion.

Or when they were silenced in a meeting.
Or when they campaigned for President.

Most were not raped by their boyfriend,
or date, or boss, but
the percentage that are
defies what we care to know.

Sexual harassment
starts and ends where, exactly?
Does HER ERA mean equality for women?

(2021)

Quatorze, ou bien plus

Kreiz Ker Seiz Breur, dans le rassemblement,
recevoir de création et du créateur,
et tout sacrifice librement donné, fleuve
infiniment libérateur de l'élan de vie, cet art :
Zizanies ou vraies vignes: laquelle es-tu ?

Cœur de mon cœur, notre fin est proche
on mettra de l'ordre dans les maisons ! Chez Yves
et pendant un temps donné, chut ! écoute !

Un mot, un regard, un seul, peut sauver !
Rions d'apprendre que dire—et peindre—c'est faire.

Les prêtres se sont nourris de cet art
où on leur a appris l'art d'être prêtre.
Regardons mosaïques au sol, peintures aux murs
et l'autel où tous s'abreuvent de poissons.

I
Je ne boirai plus du fruit de la vigne jusqu'au jour où
je boirai le vin nouveau, pensait mon père,
souffrant d'une phase avancée du cancer.
Sainte Anne, priez pour nous. Et Marie aussi.
Nous devons tous mourir, c'est un fait
mais ne pas trop y penser pour ne pas gâcher la fête.
Changera-t-il de l'eau en vin ?
La fête s'arrête nette : Jésus est condamné à mort.

II
Épancher son cœur à l'être aimé
qui ne le ferait pas, sinon pourquoi ?
La solitude ne sert qu'à porter seul
ce qu'on ne peut porter seul — ou bien —
enivrez-vous de poésie et de musique —
pour oublier pour oublier pour oublier
pollution, réchauffement, guerres et misères…
Est-ce qu'on peut les porter tous ensemble?
(Regardez là, les apôtres s'endorment à la prière).
Secousses et soubresauts soupèsent
quand Jésus est chargé de sa croix.

III
Par détermination farouche d'y arriver
qui n'est pas tombé sur sa figure?
Ah zut, mon genou ! Ah mon entorse !
Un temps de guérison s'impose où l'on
médite sa chute, mais il faut avancer. Après tout,
nous poussons comme des plantes,
une branche coupée ici, une branche qui arrive par là.
Chacun porte son lot, chacun contribue
à cette vie sur terre pour la rendre belle…
Mais Jésus tombe pour la première fois
sous le poids de ce bois de péché cosmique
sans pleurer, mais déterminé, or qu'il avait
pleuré (comme les autres) juste
avant de ressusciter Lazare.

IV
Dis-moi comment une mère est censée expliquer
cela à ses enfants ou à son entourage?
Il est blessé, crevé, Il saigne, et ce gros truc qu'il porte,
et ce cortège funeste sur ce chemin.
Où se mettre?
Je veux voir et ne pas voir.
Je veux suivre et ne pas suivre.
Mon dépassement sera entier, je reste.
Jésus rencontre sa très sainte mère,
Notre Dame de Pleine Lumière.

V
Qu'est-ce qui te booste dans la vie ?
Quel acte généreux t'a tiré d'affaire ?
Quel geste amical as-tu posé pour l'autre,
un proche ou un inconnu ?
Et Simon le Cyrène aide Jésus

parce qu'il est là au bon moment
et n'a rien d'autre à faire ce jour-là ?
Tu crois cela ?

VI
Parce que c'était lui, parce que c'était moi.
Il m'a regardée et il m'a aimée
Je le savais dans mon for intérieur.
Pour les uns journaliste, pour d'autres, artiste,
mais non, j'étais juste son amie et il
fallait lui rendre la beauté de son regard
un linge à la main, pour éponger sang et sueur,
l'eau et le sang, à l'avance, quelqu'un pour
garder cette trace, je suis Véronique,
j'essuie la Sainte Face de Jésus.

VII
À celle qui m'a oint les pieds de ses larmes
à l'autre qui m'a versé du parfum sur la tête
à celle qui m'a donné à boire
à celles qui m'ont préparé à manger
et aussi à mes autres disciples et au trois
qui m'ont vu illuminé avec Moïse et Elie,
mon cœur humain…
À ceux qui m'ont touché pour être guéri
à ceux que j'ai touché pour les guérir
aux foules pour qui j'ai béni du pain pour les nourrir
aux mariés pour qui j'ai changé de l'eau en vin
mon cœur humain…
Toutes ces belles amours humaines des chanteurs :
Quand je pense à Fernande ! Non, rien de rien !
À Bicyclette, Sarah, Un petit poisson…,
Télégramme, Ne me quitte pas !
Et je suis ici et maintenant avec les amours non réalisés,

les enfants battus, les vieux délaissés,
les études lésées, les partenaires écartés,
les pornographes et les prostituées…et aussi
le policier en danger, les militaires à risque,
Breonna Taylor et George Floyd,
Zhou Guocong et Malik Oussekine,
les enfants seuls, sans papiers, dans les trains en 1942,
les morts de la guerre de 1914,
les morts du covid 2020, 2021, 2022…
Et tout cela continue sans fin !
La veuve et l'étranger, ils les égorgent,
et l'orphelin, ils l'assassinent !
Le terrorisme existe depuis Caïn et
Jésus tombe pour la deuxième fois
par les quatre horizons qui crucifient le monde.

VIII
Nous pénétrons si mal, si peu avant,
dans le for intérieur d'autrui, disait
Gide. Comment arriver alors à consoler ?
Ajoute ton nom, et le nom de ta mère,
et le nom de tes grand-mères ici,
à côté de Marie de Magdala, Salomé, Odile,
Marcelle, Christiane, Monique, Marie-Paule,
Adèle, Louise, Marie-Amandine, Betty,
Suzanne, Simone, Viviane, Ann, Janine,
Mathilde, Doris, Lorie, Ruth et Yvonne…
pour obtenir cette consolation, et l'art de consoler :
soulager, apaiser, calmer, distraire, réconforter, remonter…
Quoi ?! Christ, ta mère ! —
en toutes ses qualités féminines de Dieu—
Jésus console les saintes femmes.

IX

J'ai les yeux rivés sur les hommes loyaux du pays,
qu'ils demeurent avec moi ;
celui qui marche dans la voie des parfaits
sera mon servant. Ce serait comme si
le 6 janvier 2021 et le 13 novembre 2015
n'avaient pas eu lieu. Ce serait comme si Notre-Dame de Paris
et la Bibliothèque d'Alexandrie n'avaient
pas brûlé. La démocratie est
une méthode de fonctionnement à plusieurs voix,
pas si différente de la Trinité, quand elle marche par
voix diverses qui se respectent et s'apprécient.
Ce monde n'est pas idéal, et sans éducation de l'humain
sur l'humain (c'est-à-dire des humanités), point de démocratie, or
la Trinité, elle, demeure d'Alpha à Omega ; point de fin possible.
Le roi David était juste, beau gosse, splendide chanteur,
son ami Jonathan loyal et brave. La monarchie peut
opérer positivement — mais la Tyrannie n'est pas de Dieu.
Liberté, Égalité, Fraternité au fond sont des valeurs chrétiennes,
(couper des têtes, non !). Servir son pays
est noble. Kennedy disait : ne demandez pas ce que votre
pays peut faire pour vous, demandez ce que vous pouvez faire
pour votre pays. Pour Sénèque, il faut prendre l'univers pour Patrie.
Ce que j'ai fait. JE SUIS LE PAIN DE VIE.
Et là, s'arrête sa réflexion,
car Jésus tombe pour la troisième fois.

X

Je sors de cette douche au savon particulier
pour aller sur le bloc opératoire
du chirurgien blessé de T.S. Eliot…? Tant qu'à faire,
revisiter Terzieff en Becket
Dans *Meurtre dans la Cathédrale*. Ou Terzieff en stop
sur la route de Compostelle chez Buñuel, pour le voir avec humour.

Ou voir *Le Festin de Babette*, dans le registre tendresse.
Dialogue des Carmélites, version opéra de Poulenc,
pour la qualité sonore…
On peut aussi lire George Herbert, qui,
comme prêtre, met son art et son être sur l'autel.
Déshabiller ma culture pour habiller Paul ?
Et Pierre vient de me renier…
Non, ce n'est pas tout à fait cela non plus. Plutôt savoir que
les lys sont habillés sans fils ni tissus, avec splendeur,
tout en s'abandonnant à
la Providence (où Judas et moi sommes proches, selon Amos Oz—
et proche du secours populaire aussi !)
Dorothy Day pensait que s'il y avait
deux manteaux dans le placard, cela faisait un de trop.
Ce je-tu de l'intimité que perçoit Martin Buber
va être préfiguré par ce partage,
Je les ai portés, portez-les bien, pense Jésus,
dépouillé de ses vêtements.

XI

Il n'y a pas que toi, tout le monde doit faire face
l'enfant sans père ni mère,
l'enfant de quatre ans dont les parents divorcent,
l'adulte qui n'en est pas un, cet enfant qui refuse de grandir,
celui qui a des tics et des tocs,
celle en situations répétées de double contrainte,
celle sous la coupe d'un pervers narcissique,
celui qui est schizophrène ou paranoïaque,
celle qui a perdu son emploi,
celui qui a perdu son amour,
celle qu'on interne (Camille Claudel)
celle prisonnière de sa santé fragile (Frida Kahlo)
celle limitée par le fait d'être femme (Emily Dickinson)
celle qu'on brûle (Jeanne d'Arc).

Dans un psaume on lit :
Tu éloignes de moi amis et proches;
ma compagnie, c'est les ténèbres.
Si la foi n'a pas les œuvres, elle est tout à fait morte,
c'est ce que dit Saint Jacques en pensant à moi,
en remémorant ce moment-ci précisément.
Je suis cloué sur ma croix un peu comme
Jésus est cloué sur la croix.

XII
Les sept dernières paroles du Christ sont sommaires :
Pardonne-leur, ils ne savent pas
Aujourd'hui tu seras avec moi
Voici ton fils / Voici ta mère
Mon Dieu, Mon Dieu, pourquoi m'as-tu abandonné?
J'ai soif
Tout est accompli
Entre tes mains je remets mon esprit.
○○○
Les dire à haute voix à mon tour, est-ce même possible?
Que signifient-elles ces paroles, pour moi?
Cette parole du larron, celle-là, je peux la dire —
Jésus, souviens-toi de moi, lorsque tu viendras comme roi.
○○○
Qu'est-ce que je comprends de ce Christ mourant sur la croix ?
en Juif accompli, il connaît la Bible comme sa poche.
Il est tout en vie, tout en relation, tout en don,
Avec son corps et son âme qui sont tout à Dieu,
Jésus meurt sur la croix.

XIII
Relever son père tombé par terre, avec de l'aide,
porter un corps qui s'enroule ou aux articulations raides,
trouver le grand-père mort, les bras étendus,

penser le corps de sa mère secouée par la mise en bière,
la grand-mère froide au fond de sa tombe…
Voici venu le tour de Jésus, ce n'est plus lui qui agit,
mais d'autres qui s'occupent de lui.
Qui osera s'en occuper ? Qui donnera son obole à Charon ?
C'est la nécessité absolue d'enterrer les morts chez Antigone…
Et peu importe combien cela coûte…
Jésus est descendu de la croix.
Et à ce moment-là,
(est-ce Péguy qui le dit ?) Marie est devenue laide.

XIV
Jésus est mis au tombeau
et c'est un jour de ténèbres
et puis un autre, quand il visite les enfers.
Mais il ne va pas y rester, aux enfers.
Jésus est mis au tombeau comme nous.
Mais il ne va pas y rester (comme nous).
Trop de vie vibrante de Dieu pour ce pan de vie,
PAIN DE VIE, comment l'enfermer ?
Ce grain cosmique, cette vie, va forcément s'éclore—
Rien ne peut le contenir et la vie est plus fort que la mort.
On voit déjà Marie-Madeleine accourir pour dire que
ce tombeau est vide.

XV
Kaddish pas dit, car il est déjà ailleurs,
aromates apportés par les femmes ne serviront pas !
Lorsque les apôtres l'entendent ils pensent : radotage de femmes.
Or Jésus trouve deux disciples sur la route vers Emmaüs
Niant encore les paroles des femmes… *Pedit evidomp* !
Korrigans moins bêtes, c'est la bénédicité qui les décolle.
Après cela, Jésus mange du poisson grillé devant les apôtres.
Les aimant, il leur ouvrit l'esprit à l'intelligence des Écritures.

On voit alors Thomas, incrédule jusqu'à
la prunelle de ses yeux, qui touche les plaies :
Non bon sang ! Il est vivant ! Resucitooooo ! Alléliuiaaaaa !

(2021-2022)

Recipe

The “Ask Carolyn”
column says —
Value each
other’s well-being
as equal to your own,
without loosing
yourself
along the way.

Choose a partner
who fits
who you are
and what you want
out of life.
You need to share
the essential.

Add ungrudging
respect
for your differences
and your right
to have them.

Then, make a
constant investment
in your mutual
happiness —
And, for God's sake, kid,
+ cross your fingers +

Oh, What is That?

Inflation nation we are still alive
we are
we are
we are us, until we are not
are we?

Your gas is mine, thanks

Fauvel, that anacronym of choice for
people trying to find a voice
amidst the un-consented sex,
chaos, ruin, and unspoken evil
(sung a-capello)
of oligarchs and trumps of all sorts
years without skills loom
thanks to the blind king

or 100 years of war
and multiple Popes at once
and the divisions and secessions

A bird came down the walk
she did not know they saw
They grabbed their knives and cut her back,
ate her, yellow, raw

Children, for the thrill —
Kirill, the name that rhymes with kill,

My cloud went with that cable, and yours,
with that bomb —
that book's gone —

NO.
MORE.
LIBRARIES.

Splendid light of Spring
Golden sunshine, O my heart,
How I miss your smile !

There is no more time
for you —or—
There is no more time
to live without you

But I do, we do, and it is hell.
We know the toll
of what is
happening and coming
but, just to rewind

I was watching CNN in Sousse (Tunisia)
when Nancy Pelosi brought down
the gavel in the House for the first time
— and there was still hope —

(we do not have enough body bags)
15,000,000 Military deaths in WW2
average age 23

25,000,000 wounded
45,000,000 estimated civilian deaths
But the real numbers are anyone's guess
admits the National World War Two
museum in New Orleans
(if they survived the 2022 tornado)
I really thought their number was
Hurricane Katrina
(Andrew, Ike, Sandy, Maria, Harvey…)

By end March 2022
half of the children in Ukraine
had become displaced persons

Meanwhile back in the midst
of the Pandemic,
"Spanish" Flu infected
500,000,000 (1/3 of the world's population)
and caught up some 50,000,000
and Covid in April 2022 had
infected close to 500,000,000 and
killed over 6,200,000 —
and was not stopping
(nor were the vaccines)

By 2023 the NYT reported
US covid deaths less than
150 a day.
OK, so is it *over* yet?

A NATO general said
(while the TV was still relatively uncensored)
that a certain Russian general had not
been able to be reached for comment

and that there could perhaps
be 20,000,000 European deaths
— if it comes to that —

And then a US general frankly
anticipated war with China in 2024.
That looks like a gaping hole
in the education budget
if you ask me—but of course you don't.

April is the cruelest month
We get that now
and Wendy C. wrote:

A Phoenician called Phlebas forgot
About birds and his business—the lot,
Which is no surprise,
Since he'd met his demise
And been left in the ocean to rot.

And Pound in *Canto* LXXVII:
For nowt so much as a just peace
That wd/ obstruct future wars
[…] has been signed.

Way to go buddy!
As the four millionth refugee drives into Europe
someone's brain bursts—
(I hope it was not yours)

And someone should bless
the waste land and
the Orthodox church and those folks that
signed the petition saying

that Jesus would stop and
smell the roses
and be a good Samaritan
and feed the hungry crowds
with two fish and some iodine pills
made in China

Zelensky, are you still there?

Prices at the grocery store
are up again this week
how much can you buy and stock
and where?

Maybe this is a poem
about 1938 and 1939
I've had a good life so
if I die now, who cares
and as for the ones that suffer
most from the wealth gap
why would they mind a
jolly little war

Whose Yacht is it?
Oh, what is that sound?

Meanwhile in Rheims,
(city of Joan of Arc,
along with Rouen, Chinon, and all)
some student was found praying
behind a closed door
and denounced
publicly on social media

denounced for praying?
Hello student world, I do this too,
ALL THE TIME
and in plain sight, but you do not see
(during your exams)
me do it. I pray if I want to
AND YOU CANNOT STOP ME
(and why should you, who even cares after all?)
What I do with my own mind is nobody's
business, in the end,
anyway, I pray you succeed
on your exams and
on everything else that counts for you

---

business is business is business
and never stops

---

breathe-pray-breathe-pray-breathe-pray-
BREATHE

---

is it a democracy if you cannot exercise
your freedom of religion behind a closed door?
Not anymore than it is not a democracy if
people are imposing their belief system upon you
via the State (ie - no abortion or forced abortion)
or trying to convert you to something
or forcing you to wear something
(my body is my own, thanks)
or taking away your capacity for thought
(my mind is my own, thanks)
Oh to hell with it, I studied APOLOGETICS
and PROPAGANDA and they are similar…
as Randall Jarrell knew
(his wet fur froze)

which makes Putin and Kirill all the more chilling,
Chillingsworth. I have not thought of *him*
for a while—one swell character study.
But I'm on Dimmesdale's side: the
hidden guilt in plain sight,
the heart that cannot have
the love it desires
for whatever reason
/ la vie en creux /
like a rare, costly, empty vase
and yet, still
so very
beautiful
Pearl
it's a wonderful life

"For your freedom and for ours
[…] stability in Europe is critically important
[…] a sacred commitment…"
said Biden in Poland, March 26
and the second month of
the Ukraine conflict begins…

Elections are coming
There are flags everywhere
And the weather has been fabulous
Predicted dryness to come
and wheat shortages
but for now it is spring
and here I sit and sing
with Lamartine
There is no happiness for me anywhere
one person is missing, and the whole world seems empty.
"Nulle part le bonheur ne m'attend […]

Un seul être vous manque, et tout est dépeuplé."
Life would be so sweet, on the sunny side of the street…

Se résigner, to be resigned to it
another day, today is gray, and raindrops
have flickered the window pane
another colleague another conflict
another pay cut (from inflation)
another tax hike (from inflation)
another year another course-grab
another train cancellation
another rejection for research funding
another cut in hours the public service is open
another two years to work before retirement
so are you going to re-elect that?

I am raw: not prepared
not hardened
definitely not fused
unprocessed, in the natural state,
and unmanufactured
untanned and undressed
undiluted and unsalted
partly refined and unrefined too,
I am crude, I lack the finishing touches,
I run around in un-hemmed trousers
Unadjusted, uncorrected, uncivilized,
(That's why this lady is a tramp)
Unripe and immature,
without skin, the flesh exposed
in this raw weather
in this raw climate
freezing cold and
worse for the wear

but don’t call me unskilled or inexperienced

I deal in raw silk
and the fabric made from such
and raw umber

(2022-2023)

The People I'm Writing This For

the people i'm writing this for don't need another poem
problem is, what else do i know how to make?
then again, a poem is better than a social media
post or an avatar's wave or a smiley face
until it isn't

the people i'm writing this for, well some
are dead now, and some will be soon,
and some are the living dead,
having never lived

and of course, the people i'm writing this for
are the people, we the people —
the people wee, as we all do,
and of course i'm writing this for me
(hey Sandy, it's about time &
Rosanna —wink, wink—)
Fables of the Self
or **in this case** foibles

the people i'm writing this for may be related
or unrelated; they may read or never read this
whatever it is. wherever we are.
the people i'm writing this for have my back
or not — backed up to the wall and screaming

the people i'm writing this for pushed me to do it
with their torture tactics, their war crimes, their novichok,
their Jamal Khashoggi and Péguy's *Saints Innocents*
and those murdered for Navalny
or the nativity of Perestroïka

the people i'm writing this for might
mix their politics and their religion, but rather subtly
so that everyone could find their own place in
tolerance

the people I am writing this for
have been leaders of something: the photogenic
Martine Aubry (at ICP), the smiling Anne
Hidalgo (at Notre-Dame Cathedral),
the Denis Mukwege of the
honorary doctorate (from Université Rennes 2),
Florence Berthout sponsoring the arts
(in her office, attempting to preserve the Boutique des Cahiers —)

the people i'm writing this for rarely win the elections
(but i wish some would) and if they did
would this be a different world?

(by the way, hats off to a few colleagues)

the people i'm writing this for are refugees
or people who are not afraid of refugees
we are all refugees on Earth, and it's going
to hell pretty damn fast
so be prepared to move

the people i'm writing this for should not
plan to solve problems by getting to the Moon or Mars

or to the town a day's horse-ride away in an automobile
that drives itself — into someone or
right off the road

the people i'm writing this for might
(on the other hand) try automatic writing and OULIPO
just taking out some letters, here or there,
surrealistically, to go with the times

Times of London / *New York Times* /
WaPo / *Chicago Tribune* / *The Atlantic* /
The Nation / *Le Monde* / *Le Nouvel Obs* / etc / etc
some real news still exists so…
we could all just leave Facebook and Twitter,
Instagram and Snapchat now
and communicate in person and in writing
and on the phone, with our real, live voices
that might not be heard in China

but, do you still remember how to write by hand?

(2022-2023)

Breonna

Breonna, soon

may you be

vindicated

more than an

ekphrasis

on the cover of magazines

you could have been somebody's mother, maybe

like the mother of

Wilton Gregory or Serena Williams

or

every name
that exists in
American English

and we are just saying those names out loud
the hey mary's will follow
after these pass
between my fingers
holding the fountain pen
at a thirty or forty degree angle
so the ink effectively
flows smoothly on the paper
(or on Thomas Jefferson's desk)
like blood
or like the beads
of a never ending rosary
that will someday
redeem my country
deem my country so
to be redeemed
may it be
by Breonna Taylor
tis of thee George Floyd
my country

John Taylor
Albert Martin
Earl Little

Abram Smith
Eli Ladd
George Scott
George Ward
Henry Smith
James Dillard
James Jenning
Thomas Henderson
Thomas Shipp

Robert Alexaner

Charles Allen

James Ball

Frank Ballard

William Bell

Alexander Bell

Luther Billings

Dennis Blackwell

Andy Blount

Green Boman

Joseph Brake

Thomas Brooks

Curtis Brown

Charles Brown

Robert Bruce

Garfield Burley

George Call

William Chambers

Robert Clark

Samuel Clay

Walter Cole

John Collar

Nimrod Cross

Patrick Crump

Balli Crutchfield

John Davis

Thomas Devert

M Donald

York Douglas

L.C. Dumas

Jeff Ellis

Medgar Evers
    Addie Mae Collinns
        Cynthia Wesley
            Carole Robertson
                Carol Denise McNair

Michael Brown
    Treyvor Martin
        Eric Garner
            Maurice Gordon
                Ahmaud Arbery
                    James Baker

and so the steps to the Capitol continue…

my country Malcolm X
my face Emmet Till
Black Lives Matter

hey
mary
full of good looks
and tender hugs
the lord is with you
and your child looks awesome
lovely mary
nurturer of god
and the good
pray for us as we err
now and at the end
amen

(2020-2022)

If Charles Péguy's *Jeanne* were an American Movie

It would begin with a brilliant scene written by George Bernard Shaw, in medias res outside New Orleans, with Baudricourt shouting, "Am I a cowboy?'' as they tried to save people during Hurricane Katrina, for longer than the first twenty minutes, before cutting to some early film footage from *Joan the Woman*: "The time has come for thee to expiate thy sin against me." Of course this would be with acknowledgment to Cecil B. De Mille, Jeanie Macpherson, and Geraldine Farrar.

During the next ten minutes, they found money to sponsor legislation against opioids, with some Cocteau gestures, and the occasional voice-over by Madame Simone. And there would still be a Shakespeare quotation, and an allusion to Robert Southey and Brecht's Joan in the meat-packing plants in Chicago. Then there was a flashback to Donremy (in Saskatchewan) where Joan would be sweetly sleeping under pink felt sheets in the winter and a blue jean quilt—no visible red Levis tag (because it would be made by hand locally, not in a Bangladeshi sweatshop).

And Joan would be dressed uniquely in red in bed in her red flannel nightie (sure, that was a nod to Margaret Atwood; but Joan would never be taken [sic!] for a handmaid). By day, her red t-shirt and red jeans are highlighted by pink socks and black sneakers And a black jacket. She would look masculine and feminine at the same time—as in real life. In at least one scene she would wear a pussy hat.

Angela Davis would play the great Jeanne for most of the film, though occasionally Barbara Streisand or Cher would step in, marching for Civil Rights in the 1960s—Protesting Vietnam—shouting for

Women's Rights the same decade—and 50 years later—and directing protesters during multiple manifestations of Black Lives Matter—(she helped paint the street on BLM plaza in DC, of course). Then Mark Twain would make an anachronistic guest appearance to hand Angela-as-Joan a wreath.

Wearing her mask, she would go to the border to mourn children who died in detention from covid, and then she went looking to find their parents. After which she placed Twain's wreath on the tomb of Heather Heyer. And then, after electric-biking cross-country, attended a Gay Pride march in Seattle.

After her attempt to shout at the judge in the trial of the Chicago Eight, Joan was played by a Phillis-Wheatley-look-alike at her own trial juried by every male that received a Trumped Pardon in 2020. Her counsel was led by Christine Blasey Ford, and they stayed as close to Quicherat as possible, so the movie never seemed long, but it went on and on. OK, you knew there was no happy end, right?

Chess Records revived to make the soundtrack album, with music by Armstrong, Muddy Waters, and Jay-Z working in Joan's army—with "My Power ''by Chika as general theme song underlying the whole film produced, with no hesitation, by Spike Lee — who still plans to visit the *Boutique des Cahiers*.

(2020-2023)

Vatican II Soundtrack

(Live Long and Prosper)

cherish

if a picture paints

the moment

i wake up

i say

a little prayer

that's what

friends are for

you make

me feel like a

natural

Diptyque

un esprit comme Romy
(moins d'hommes à l'appui)
un esprit germaniste
une liberté
et des principes
fleur bleue

le soleil de la pièce
briller ou peur de ne pas briller
dans la forêt
la plus brillante
fleur bleue

invoquer un oiseau,
une rose, l'éveil d'un enfant,
chaque instant savouré
fleur bleue

*

vie d'attente absurde
de vie toute faite
il pleure dans mon cœur
comme il pleut sur la ville
à ne pas rompre
à ne pas vivre
fleur mauve

des projets
le temps qui file
un ailleurs, une allure : non atteints
un but dans la vie ?
fleur mauve

En attente
de Dieu
de fleur bleue
et *Waiting for Godot*
fleur mauve

The cattle are lowin

(a postcard from Michigan)

oh say can you see
Momma cryin singin the national anthem?
you playin on the swingset
and catching insects
to feed the neighbor's turtle
I pwedge awegience to
Earrrrrl!? You lilac!
Doug and Tim huggin him
shots and more shots
dreamin of being shot through the glass
like Jaurès but not knowin bout him
in the glass house with nine, yes nine
sliding glass doors and windows everywhere
Nine, and dreamin of violence on violence
everybody shootin somebody
Georgie Bobby Martin Johnny Malcolm
the whole political and societal spectrum
Vietnam Mommy Mommy
guess what happened at school today?
Mommy why dew you haf to wurk?
nine times neun is 81. No Lorna please don't go!
wat iz Θis International Teacher's Alphabet?
cant yu spel Mrs. Wells?
For civics history and government see
The Flinstones The Jetsons
Peanuts holiday specials
Captain Kangaroo and Sesame Street
The Big Valley Mash Laugh-In

Saturday Night Live The Wizard of Oz
Frosted Flakes and the war dead for breakfast
Bicentennial Celebrations my arse
(in the Bible Belt I said butt)
but had already read about Lady Chatterley's
Come on dAowWn, you are the next contestant on
the New Price is Right!
(which ring from hell were they referring to?)
Motown Uptown and Civil Whites
riots from the depths of my ignorance
and not even from the ghetto, child
well, not ghetto on our side of the family
except for the heroin'd uncle —
no I didn't say heroic
though maybe he was in his way
Divorce   Divorce   Divorce
Did you? The Jew? No, the unfaithful dude
the Jew I kept, and loved him best
even though he was dispossessed
my mother had 8, but I was content with two
men, you just can't trust them
but her best gin games were with husband number one
(he always signed his letters "Abyssinia")
cards that is, for booze see husband
number two
and though you ate gefilte fish
and could say you were meshuggnah
to an uncle with numbers on his arm
barbed wire was somethin used in the prairies
to keep the cows in
somethin that stabbed you in the weddin finger
when you were less than ten
stop cryin dammit why do you always have to keep
climbin that fence when

I told you not to!
of course it's bleeding
stab the flag
free, the cows low
Frida Kahlo
I didn't know
but Ogden Nash
Was pure pizash
Por exemplo
"The cow is of the bovine ilk;
One end is moo, the other, milk."
And what's his name in the Institute of Arts
with the portrait of Henry Fuckin Ford
Please assemble me home, give me a numba
By day I make the cars, by night I make the bars
nice and gentle, ease that cue-stick
put the 8-ball in the corner and the winner breaks
Tie a yellow ribbon round the old oak tree
Hostages? Of what? Where?
In which suburban sprawl?
Don't change dicks in the middle of a screw,
vote for Nixon in '72
Heard of RACs but not much
knowledge on Sputnik
and Laïka woulda been my heroine if only
I'd a known HER
instead nightmares about bein
hijacked by Russians
comin in warships to our backyard
asked to volunteer to go to the moon
second grade kids told
we'd all become astronauts
on TV 9.9.66 Star Trek then Space 1999
not to mention Momma's 30th birthday 1969

Beam you up baby I ain't been to de moon yet
and sista you gotta know you ain't never gonna go
unless you turns into de moon goddess
in which case let's have a vote on the ERA
no it does not stand for the era
of Republican america
(And Republican don't mean républicain)
Good vibrations drivin the '77 red chevette
(rhymed with Daddy's red corvette, right?)
and Kathy's beat up Mustang
with Beatles cassettes
Mary in the sky with diamonds
I got a gal in Bronson Methodist Hospital
but the church is Baptist, don't ya know?
KKKKKKKcollege, Miller Auditorium
Boiling pot and Celeryville
Dad's 8-track tapes in the yellow tri-hull
on Indian Lake (without the Injuns)
but the Lake house had the boys' stage coach bed
and saloon doors for the kitchen just in
case one little two little three portaged
the arboratum and burial place
Malcolm's dad was killed in Lansing
his momma spent some 26 years in Kalamazoo
Take me back to city of big shoulders
majestic billboards on Lake Michigan
Every Marlbero Man's life in all its depth
is a collage of all his relationships
St Thomas, St Thomas the Apostle
can we still believe in the American Dream?
I-94 between Gary and Chicago
keep your eyes on the road
and watch out for the trucks
Boo can you please roll the window down

the smoke is really bothering me
when I grow up I wanna be the total woman
like Marabel Morgan
and greet my man
Lawfully Wedded Husband
when he comes home
by opening the front door
dressed in saran wrap so
he'll run after me
and we'll make lewd love
under the kitchen table.
(p.s. why isn't my momma like that?)
(p.p.s. what do you mean Emma Bovary? who's she?)
All aboard Amtrack!
No kidding the train used to stop
in Vicksburg on its way
to Port Huron then Toronto?
Did it ever stop in London? (Ontario, Stupid)
Almost out of adolescence
a dog named Becky went on some fugue
got herself date-raped and returned
My personal is political
and how do you eat mannerdly
in a McDonalds just tell me?
how should I hold my hamburger?
how should I lick my fingers?
Our Bodies Our Selves
Cookeville she's from Cookeville TN
Valley Authority Mind you and check Psalm 23
every valley shall be exalted
with biscuits and gravy for breakfast
Pass the grits Uncle Jess.

(2004)

Beyond Control

First you are just browsing
through the museum
or the pottery fair

and then you notice that
you have swooned — and
it's happened before

you had any control
over your reaction
or your emotions

which are now entirely
unrestrained and unchecked —
the inside of that

hand-crafted elegant
bowl exactly matches
the color of the potter's

eyes. Do you see
the form of that tea pot
where the handiwork is

exquisite. Or those rounded
spherical shapes—those colors and
textures like waves, so smooth you want

to touch, though you cannot
purchase for your tiny space,
but the artist still comes

and stands next to you,
observing and hovering,
while chatting like some angel

of annunciation, and now
you know you are having it —
the aesthetic orgasm

and you want
it to happen
again and again

(2022)

Pantheon

I. Marcelle Dale

La vie n'a pas d'âge.
La vraie jeunesse ne s'use pas
On a beau l'appeler souvenir,
On a beau dire qu'elle disparaît,
On a beau dire et vouloir dire que tout s'en va,
Tout ce qui est vrai reste là.

Jacques Prévert

When
she retired
at Lux Esto

they gifted her a chair
she had never been department chair
but you would not know it by looking at her hair
long and flowing while she stood sewing
gleaming words into
a tapestry of minds and hearts

héron serviable

she signed off her last
class with a poem by Cros
"Le hareng saur" — how dry
and witty that was: what we got
from her was bub- bling champagne
(and tears) and we were
all her children -

petits, petits, petits.

II. Aunt Eileen

Under the Michigan Avenue bridge, next to the spot where Du Sable's trading post once stood, twice yearly you used to be able to take Eileen's Polluted Waterways Tours. Reservations and payment in advance required. Watch out for Eileen in the red beret, chatting up the Wendella boat man and the first arrivals. Did you have time for breakfast? Did you bring your windbreaker? A day out gets chilly, spring and autumn, and there is a spell on the Lake.

At seven o'clock, Eileen would catch the El from Evanston. Later, when she was older and her knees couldn't take the stairs, she would taxi it: a rare ride to town. The North Side was not on those tours, and don't plan on seeing the Bahá'i Temple. Instead, think sewage and stench. That's what the 72-mile-long tours were about. Did you bring your lunch? Acid rain would be one subject of conversation, and the speakers, clad in jeans or cords and good rain gear, would point out the high levels of pollutants in the water and what harm was caused. Binoculars can be useful for noticing pipes from which waste is dumped directly into the river.

Ozone depletion, deforestation, solid waste, solar energy: water was not the only concern in the house on East Maple Ave. in Wilmette where stacks of tracts about the environment covered all surfaces, even the maps of the woman who had a B.A. in cartography and made the best buckwheat pancakes on earth. How did her alumni friends react to her interior decorating scheme? They knew of the Polluted Waterways Tours, but what of the Girl Scouts, the trip to Mexico, her two adopted children, and her mother's activism?

Look at those graineries and their silos (Demuth has painted some such). Did you bring your camera? And those car corpses piled high. See the Water Reclamation District plants and the steel mills. The sides of the river were of all colors, and often black. But over the years the smell decreased. The perceptible improvements the Tours brought could be smelt. Fish, yes, there were some, mostly catfish.

All through the 70s and 80s, a day out on the water. The polluted waters for 8 hours. On April 27, 1991, you will get a tan or a burn. Aunt Eileen, 81, will still ask the same questions. Did you bring your hat? The speakers will address pollution abatement and current environmental problems. Abandoned industrial sites will still be polluting, and the run-off still going straight into the river.

Your aunt is a strange bird, my father said to my mother. After one visit when she was even more vocal than usual, he said he didn't want to have her back. We lived far enough away that we didn't need to see her much. But it was hard to resist her Polluted Waterways Tours.

(2005)

III. Robert Penn Warren

Nobody does it quite like you, old Œdipus
You didn't sleep with your Black Mammy—
You interviewed her instead.
You were a seer, and you took your stand.

(2019)

IV. Jeanne Peeters, sfx

No one knew her for her poetry
and with the use of words
all the testimonies agree
she was spare
but of condensed meanings

she was a zen master
whose communication was
focused and well-honed
with those ticks
of her head, her agitated hand,
her polo shirts
(she was not a sharp dresser)
but oh that smile!

Her nephew described her
as a businesswoman
brisk and efficient
administrating budgets
she was in the business
of building projects and
maintenance while
attending to intendance
caring for all and watching
the children of others
eat well and grow strong.

Yes, in the business of love
for some 50 years
in one city
in one neighborhood
in one school
in many lives
in one life.

(2019)

V. L'Experte

i.m. Anne Mounic

Sage, trouvant manière de combiner Claude
Vigée, Emily Dickinson, Geoffrey Hill et
Edith Stein, les poètes de guerre et leurs muses,
Passeuse, en montrant son tempo, ses couleurs…

— The Who et Elton John chantaient *Pinball Wizard,*
enfant traumatisé, aveugle, sourd-muet,
qui savait jouer uniquement par senteurs,
renvoyant la bille vers le haut, par l'action
de mouvements gracieux et rapides du poignet —

Et il y avait aussi *Flipper le dauphin*,
où l'observation comptait autant que
le geste et le mouvement. Par ses sauts
l'heureux animal montrait les chemins.

Comme personne, Anne, un jour de janvier,
prit la parole à Strasbourg et fit résonner,
par sa bille, chaque cloche poétique.
Ce tintement musical était sa force,
experte, habile, (temporel), tempérée…

(22-2-2022)

VI. Olympe de Gouges

It seems she read the Magna Carta too:
some lines in *Rights of Women* sound very similar.
But then, some lines in Shakespeare sound like the Bible.
And even *The Englishwoman* ran an article on
Magna Carta and women in 1915.
Only Greta Thunberg seems to know
where the world will be in 2080.

VII. The People's Prof

"Your style is too pedestrian"
said Besterman
and that's how John fell into
The Profession
getting published anyway.
In contrast to his peers
who could seem rather vain,
his own long list of publications merely
made him seem more humane.
Steadfast MLA conference attender
a GI-Bill man from upstate New York
who survived World War II in Panama
"my Mother was French, my Father was Greek
and I'm 100% American" said he.
In World War I his dad fought to earn citizenship.
As a kid, he confessed
to the alcoholic priest,
and, made a habit of it
since it seemed to encourage him.
Named as the first RC
to his first job at Indiana University
where kosher food was rare in the late 1950s
blacks were bad
and sexologists somehow got away with it.
His hankering for country music
definitely a plus at Indiana
since he defended Pius XII and the Jews
on University Radio in 1963.
N. for Nicholas
and what generosity he showed
even at Boulogne-sur-Mer
quoting Rousseau at meals

to encourage the endless
procession of All-But-Dead
dissertation students along
(first his own, then other people's students).
His only son played guitar and sang
and jumped into traffic, dying in an auto accident.
Then there was his intellectual son
Charlie J., sharp young man, black,
first job in Oregon or somewhere where tolerance
sank, and he committed suicide.
The people's prof told me, some 30 years later,
he still prayed for this fellow and his son every night.
Pappas21@aol.com
is the way he concluded
and vehement Voltairian letters
to the parish, to the people who sold him the rickety refrigerator,
to the people who wrote D'Alembert with a small d,
as though it were a question of defending Democracy,
John wrote to anyone
who needed to straighten up and fly right.

(2019)

VIII. Grams

The Perfume Lady
she was to many people
To me she was an elegant fragrance
of distilled living.

(2019)

IX. Mathilde Panoff

Du jardin de sa grande mère à ENS, rue d'Ulm,
de la gare d'Alfortville, chaque jour le train

arrivant Gare de Lyon pour aller vers le Quartier
Latin, qu'elle parlait comme le grecque, puis Harvard.

Et en résidence le brassage préparant l'Agrég,
heures de bibliothèque et rencontres autres —
avec celle fraîchement arrivée du Michigan,
érudite de la Bible et, accessoirement,

la littérature anglaise, thème et version.
Pierre Roy un point de départ d'amitié,
une discussion de trois heures dans
un couloir souterrain du métro Châtelet —

cœur pur, cœur blessé, enseignante avec scrupules,
rires de connaissances et innocences mêlées
affection débordante, réceptions si chaleureuses
la montagne selon Rousseau, ainsi que l'éducation

l'écoute, le don généreux, l'idée qui change tout,
le mot juste en toute circonstance, l'empathie en plus.
Sans l'éducation que j'ai reçu d'elle (quand on
bouquinait ensemble pendant des séances de

huit heures à Beaubourg—sa concentration intense
et ces discussions…), aurais-je pu terminer ma thèse ?
Mais elle n'a pas terminé la sienne, et sa vie, terminée
à trente-huit ans, est une tragédie d'éternelle jeunesse.

Sa brillante intelligence de cœur a surpassé tous
ceux de ma génération que j'ai appelé amis : jamais
était-il question de montrer à l'autre qu'il n'en savait rien,
mais avec douceur et finesse lui faire faire la découverte…

Yours

Ton rire en moi comme un sanglot
Tes yeux en moi comme des étoiles
Ton approbation comme des cerfs dans la forêt
Tes intuitions de génie un paradisier

Ton regard en moi comme un océan
Tes mots en moi comme de l'encens qu'on respire
Tes rebondissements des collines à grimper
Tes projets des levers de soleils

Tes lettres une promesse
Tes regards compassion
Ta cuisine une musique de fête
Ta présence un cadeau

Tes reproches un feu purifiant
Ton sourire un baume

(2022)

On Academia

1

Your lipstick

It seemed false, so different from my grandmother's.
She wore hers every day. I could watch
her apply first liner, then two shades.
An artist, she could make her lips fuller.
Useful it was, for standing all day while selling
lipstick and perfume and looking beautiful.

But your lipstick is about power.
And what are you so worried for?
The power plays are all yours—
I will only write this about you
(and the way you work)
without your name.

(2005)

2

Soaring

Not albatross
but Canadian goose
honking up a storm

wings unfurled to
fly in formation
above
the snowy landscape
our image in V
reflected
in the crystal lakes
cruising just above you now
catch some wind
from my tail feathers

(2005)

3

The Grant

Goofy Dripdrap spent 5 days writing the project with occasional collaboration from 2 partners so approx 40 hours of work (and a certain amount of stress). The grant (if granted) amounted to 3000. So working at 10 an hour would be 400 already, but Goofy usually makes about 1200—> so the grant money is not really so generous: you must already cut 1/3 for overhead. And, Goofy was working significant overtime to get it done because teaching and other stuff had not just stopped which is always the case, always the date is just tomorrow or next week…except that time long ago when Goofy spent no time on personal research for three months writing a significant complex project (for nothing) or that other time when Goofy protested with the unions in the streets for three months (for nothing).

The 40 hours paid off (so to speak). Awarded 1000 you might say Goofy broke even. So how is it that Goofy remained broke?

(2012-2022)

4

Lizard Hotel

As the young lizard extended his path
into the Hotel Ortler dining room we laughed.
Last night he was strutting by the pool
yet mountain views seemed more than he could stand.
Some call shifty wobbling creatures reptiles,
but lizards have all our sympathies. I
tried to catch one once, but held her tail instead—
her leopard spots I could not understand.
This lizard line has lived in Dorf Tirol
like a tradition of several thousand years.
Another sat on a rock wall near a bench
where the stones of the temple are not for sale.
Off Falkner way at Brunnenburg a lizard
upheld me: what I did was small but good.

(2015)

5

Marketing Literature
(WTF else can you do with it?)

She's the hawker of American Literature
and if she can sell it, the fruits of narrative
are superior to the fruits of the loom,
and a few other things besides, or so she says.

You can almost see her trying to
shout over the tradesman in the next booth
on market day (add a Brooklyn accent
until the end of this stanza):

What kind ya want? what kind ya want?
Hispanic American? Sandra Cisneros
Asian American? Amy Tan
Jewish American? Cynthia Ozick
African American? Langston Hughes, Richard Wright,
James Baldwin, Gwendolyn Brooks,
Margaret Walker, Toni Morrison, Rita Dove…
You need any mustard with that?
Comic Book American? Tarzan and Superman
Short Story American? Tillie Olsen and Grace Paley
American American? Joyce Carol Oates
Catch-you-by-your-toes American? *The Confederacy of Dunces*
If you dona like what I'm selling go to
Leslie Fielder's stand for
Northerns Westerns
Easterns and Southerns.

Or she's a sweet waitress in a Mom & Pops Restaurant
trying to gently guide you through the menu:
Honey, how about a dapple of Flannery
O'Conner to top off that Faulkner-Gaines
cupcake? And you, Sugar, would you
like a Robert Penn Warren Soda? Or would you
rather enjoy a Robert Lowell Tea?
No Dear, we only serve the Steinbeck and
Hemingway Cocktails during Happy Hour.
Today's Special is Modernism — Eat in for 10
or 9.50 Ready for Take Out.
It's a bit high on the spice,
but you'll acquire a taste for it.

(2019)

6

Untied States
(on teaching American Civ in Langues Étrangères Appliquées)

It's late capitalism while *L'Invention de l'Année 2018* is closer to what I wish could be my *modus operandi* but that election justifies and vindicates any and every American-bashing comment I've ever heard

And believe me, living overseas you hear all kinds of anti-American remarks. People wonder why the USA went to war with Iraq in 2003 when there were no 'weapons of mass destruction'. But there are weapons of mass distraction.

(2019)

7

Gray Areas

"By power of the authority
Vested in me" said Hannah
        But by whom was it vested?
        Did you mean invested?
Repeating it, again and again,
The sliding wipe of the hand,
        Perhaps slightly too fast,
        Holborn sweeping you forward
Like the Am Ex swiped through
The charge account
        Charging it was. Tab up
        The short-term and the long-term loans.
Years later, looking grayer, raincoat vintage 1960,
I saw her one rainy day next to the Seminary co-op.
        Invested power (not quite) gone.

(2003)

8

To Tench or not to Tench

> 'She had no time to read, but if she had, she imagined that she might reread *The Power and the Glory*. That semester she kept thinking of herself as Madame Tench. She felt so much like the dentist who kept pushing everything off in a world that was crumbling around her. She also felt her students might nickname her Ms. Carp and that they were beginning to see her classroom as a penitentiary.'

Jane stopped reading and looked up at the creative writing teacher, who replied with authoritative fervor:

> 'No no no. That's not it. You need to write it like Greene combined with Bernanos and then simply let the character of the teacher be a Mme Tench. But never mention either author's name. It's for the reader to figure that out. In fact, you are not obliged to use the name Tench. It could be too much of a give-away. The newspapers have just begged for the great French University novel. They notice that novels about the academy exist in Britain and the US, but not in France. Britain has several novels by David Lodge, Zadie Smith's *On Beauty* and Byatt's *Possession*. The States landed Randall Jarrell's *Pictures from an Institution* and *The Marriage Plot* by Eugenides. But in France . . it's an open slot, you really should run with this narrative…'

In her head, Jane vowed that she would, but now she would be on her own for the writing, the course was ending, and the teacher was retiring. She had enjoyed most classes with this professor, though some scolding had put her off. It was time to take things into her own hands. She began the plot line again. Her mother was also a teacher and she had heard far too much about the inner workings of life on several campuses in France since the 1990s. As to the name Tench, she would keep it. No one she knew was still reading much, and it was unlikely, she felt, that anyone would pick up the reference. And anyway, it gave a bit of punch to the way she wanted the narrative to run. Tench had numerous evocative sonorous possibilities: clenching one's teeth, being in a trench, sitting on a bench. Just like the combination of the words university and reform, nothing very positive emitted from the sounds of tench, whether in a whisper or a full-throttled and hopeless scream.

(2018)

What is European?

A

Paris Blues
(January 6, 2015)

Paris Blues
Feast of Kings.
Notre-Dame unlit.
Before her, Putin's effing X-Mass tree shining blue.
Île de la Cité wrapped in a giant Coca-Cola advert plastered
over the Quai des Orfèvres.
I'm lost.
Where is the Sainte Chapelle?
This city looks like Hell at six
in the morning.

(2015)

B

Magna Brexit

In 1215 'The Body wished to rule the head'
at the British Library at the Magna Carta exhibit in 2015.
Ever since, it seems like Britain cannot wait to undo itself.
But have the descendants of William Penn fared worse?

'For the protection of all citizens' wrote Kurt Weill
and Jay-Z went to Salisbury because his ancestors not so protected
But in 1976 the Magna Carta was in the US
'to celebrate the centenary of American Independence'.

Magna Brexit: oxymorons abound. Someone's
tongue has twisted, more than once, and more than one—
from democracy and human rights
to walls protecting whites and cages for children.

The Rights of Man (1940), the Four Freedoms (1941), and the
Universal Declaration of Human Rights (1948) with *habeas corpus*.
Free to speak, free to p(r)ay your own way,
free from poverty, free from fear—
Free to hope things will be better next year.

(2019)

C

1989 in 2022

Bicentenary celebration of note
And I *was* there
Much more European
(and American)
than I knew then
Ben Franklin's Paris places

so close to where tourists
now go for *macarons*
The *DÉCLARATION DES DROITS*
DE L'HOMME ET DU CITOYEN
one could quote
at that time

and now
in this time
it’s almost all
travesty macaroons

Not bourgeois

I am not bourgeois (thanks for reminding me, cher Jacques Brel),
and I don't belong to any one clan —
I am not even French, although I like what Charles Péguy says about
them (and maybe even most of what he says about me).
I am not a citizen of any one country, but think universal,
think heaven.
I am not Anglican, Protestant, Catholic, Jewish or Muslim,
and I like the Dalai Llama, and Hindus do not eat animals.
I am not exactly who people say I am — and politicians
do not understand me.
I am not white and I am not materially wealthy, nor do I wish to be.
I am not happy about air pollution, solid wastes, the Kyoto protocol.
I am not in touch with the "what would Jesus drive" movement.
I am not concerned with a woman's spotless reputation, and virginity
and wedding-gifts are rather unnecessary if you are trying to
give birth to God-in-you.
I am not a man or a woman, so to speak.
I am amazed at avid readers, people with long memories, and
people who use words.
I am the kind of person you could find reading a good book, if I
weren't so busy with other matters.
I am the kind of person who might stop attending to urgent matters
so as to read a good book.
I am the kind of person who still thinks that poetry at its best is
superior to most prose.

I am enchanted by music and song, and all beauty is amazing to me.
I am constantly hoping that you will prefer art to war (instead of
the contrary).
I am not what you expect, nor what you imagine me to be.
I am who I am, says God.

(2007)

The Lady of the House

You can enter the Cluny again,
the courtyard, exterior architecture
with archeological finds,
gaze raptly at jewelry worn on some
body of the 14th century with
interest and joy
maybe they were great
grandchildren of troubadours,
or wives of those who fought
next to Joan of Arc at Orléans

you can almost catch the scent of
flowers in the unicorn tapestry
so go early, when the museum opens
and take some time to meditate with
the Lady of the House
in The Love Room

Et parleray des six sens,
cinq dehors et ung dedans
qui est le cuer.
Jean Gerson, 1402

The lady loved her animals
monkeys, rabbits, lions, unicorns
and they loved her
devotedly. *Mon seul désir*
whose motto?

And when she enjoys one sense, they
in turn, see, listen, taste
touch and smell: I do believe
I saw a cat
with a flehman response
and there's such
emotion in that
Unicorn's eyes

If you didn't know better
you'd almost think you were
in paradise
or at high mass
after a touch of gifted peace
in Notre Dame Cathedral
when the incense rises
while the choir sings
and the organ plays
during the Eucharist

En un instant, mon cœur fut
touché et je crus.
Paul Claudel

And now you look closely at
the sixth tapestry
Mon seul désir
like an epiphany
where the animals express
all their senses all at once

love quickens every sense

(May 2022)

Riffing on Yourcenar

tu sauras que
ton âme voyage
comme au fond de
mon cœur et que rien
ni le temps
ni l'âge
n'empêcheront
jamais ce que
j'ai vu et appris de
toi

que la beauté
du monde qu'a pris
ton visage et
ta douceur continuent
à briller au fond
de moi et à m'inspirer

que le temps de
paroles a laissé trace

tes luttes, espoirs,
peines et projets,
ma pensée accompagne
que ce soit de loin
ou de près

Balbutiements (from student days)

Images of May (Chicago, 1984)

determined violets poke their faces at quieter sidewalks
and glittering brick stone shelters them from the
smattering of faces moving
through the loop. priestly collars rub with bearded cigars
and perfumed, high-heeled rich. the elderly defense-
lessly totter against the flow.
at intersections all dodge packages and briefcases. shoppers
shove to catch sardined buses coming too slowly from
a stream of endlessly polluting
traffic. feet are smacking pavement. waves of shoulders
bounce up and down. a saxophonist sounds from a bridge,
playing musical competition to the guitar across the way;
music cannot calm the terse movements of hurried
businessmen on their way to lunch. they must choose,
somehow, from a myriad of restaurants. boul-mich? scandinavian?
crêpes? enchiladas? a popcorn vendor?
oh-weep, weep-oh from the whistles under the el tracks,
somewhere a guard snitches his brown-bag lunch
beside a building directory.
"yes, that's right ma'am, the 23rd floor."
wisps of bells hang near the wrigley building, their peals
blending, rendering them
indistinguishable.

sitting on the sidewalk a dirty face has hands
outstretched, begging.
construction hardwood surrounds another building
in a steel embrace. hard hats lazily watch the
passing images. next to the river a man has found a patch
of green grass to snooze on. drugs
are being exchanged in a parking lot.
"did you see that idiot dressed up like a gorilla?"
"fresh roses here!"
a mounted policeman guides his horse along the magnificent
mile incongruously towering over taxis and gold-coast cars.
an occupied stroller waits perilously close
to the curb.

(1984)

Thé à la menthe

Michigan's winter has begun
and in the American earthenware cup
swirls the steaming sugared brown-green liquid;
a sweet taste of heat,
and now the plate of cookies passed…

Focusing from the T.V. soccer match in Spanish
to a quiet conversation…

soon the photograph album comes out and we are travelling.
(We have made more than one voyage together —
and several without my noticing until after the fact.)

Ah! There himself in his prime and ambitious,
a pattern of steadfast excellence from year to year.
And look, the vacation in Spain and his young wife

wearing fresh polka dots. The sunlight was strong —
their son happy to play with a puppy.

Nineteen sixty-one
schooling to be repeated… language to be conquered…
Courage required. (In the land of the free foreign
diplomas not recognized.)

The plate of cookies passed again,
and her home-made recipe changed
to low-sugar since his surgery.

Here the *maître* of my high school days
with infinite charm in the accent he will never lose
advising me to *prendre la vie du bon côté…*

And I am melancholy because even
his *moustache* has turned gray, eventually.

(1985)

Blessed are the Urban Poor
(Election Day, 1984)

Groping hand touching wire
groping, digging deeper…
scraped dirty nails
against cold metal searching
for food.
Papers for warmth…
On to the next can.

Green bench for bed
hard wood slats;

the bolts stick one's back
and when it's cold
no warmth to be found.
Or,
one could sleep on one of those
decorative benches —
the kind at bus-stops where
a religious organization pays
for a verse from the Bible to be printed
on the back for all to see.

On bus some clod quips:
"See bum sleeping with Jesus saves insurance."

Two plastic Jewel bags hold
a precious quilt of newspapers and patched clothing,
a crust of McDonald's burger —
perhaps a bottle

Where the train tracks fork out an isolated triangle
of bushes
                    one can build a small
                                        fire and camp out
relatively unnoticed.

          Small warmth for November.
Whose hearts are calloused?

(1984)

The Fly

Is it the flight of the bumblebee?
No, but a fly to keep me company.

He buzzes round my foot and chair
While I observe his fuzzy blue hair.

His path in flight's a peculiar maze
Never charting one definite way
And reminiscent of my own musing haze
As life leaps on from day to day.

(1987)

agrarian grammarian

I lurked behind the barn
Whose cows were lowing
By themselves at the moon;
Who lowed what where?

Stealthing through the haystacks
I lost the forgotten needle
Point to point
I promise the last time is this time
... or don't I?

(1986, with fond memories of 5, rue de l'école de Médecine)

Breakfast at Ruth's

Toasted raisin blood
bagel crumbs and strokes of cream cheese
paint the white plate
which every morning holds that which
paints my palate.

(1984)

Pour Françoise (à Bordeaux)

En un tout petit instant
je t'ai revue
brûlée du chocolat chaud sur ma langue
goût du discours inachevé
longue soirée
à pied traversant le pont
des quartiers déserts
magasins fermés et maisons endormies
ville noire où seules
nos têtes font tête-à-tête,
lumières "at large"
nos pensées dansent dans les rues
désertées.

(1982)

The Poetry Man

> "Yet with these April sunsets, that somehow recall
> My buried life and Paris in the Spring…"

Haunting the Odeon quarter
in a brown trench coat
he'll sneak up to you.
You walk by
he'll look you in the eye
and say, "Aimez-vous la poésie?"

How to reply? If you say *oui*
he'll thrust typed pages from his briefcase
toward you and ask you to buy
(40 francs for 10 pages).

If you say *non*, you lie…
Another unsatisfactory way
to handle the situation
is to shrug.

On a different day, he'll be lying in wait
at the foot of the stairs, rue Dubois
in a brown tweed jacket, puffing a pipe.
Now with a simple leather portfolio,
head tilted to one side and an intellectual jaunt
he feigns to walk past you…

Only to do a right angle turn,
and leaning into your face he insists,
"Ça vous intéresse, la poésie ?"
Again you avoid his candid stare.
Is it too much like looking into the mirror?

(1986)

L'Appel Normand

Cerner le chemin ensoleillé
Qui monte et descend,
S'enroule autour des champs
Au-delà des toits de maisons normandes
Recouverts de chaume et d'iris.

Chemin ombré de silhouettes
Des troncs d'arbres, de buissons jaunâtres
Et du sumac rouge : buisson ardent.

Chemin de petites églises villageoises
Entourées de tombeaux des vies passées…
Quel chemin?
Souffle une légère brise et murmure un ruisseau.

Vaches couchées dans la verdure
Et au loin un fermier suit sa machine
Qui tire d'une chaîne ses pommiers, pour les secouer.
Comme des balles vertes et dorées
Les pommes tombent là-bas par douzaines.

(1989)

A Different Artist

for Lesley

You created something
and then lived within the confines of its form;

You created, and it moved, thought, acted, loved, played,
accepted or rejected, of its own free will;

You created it to create anew, to give birth in turn,
to have its own art forms.

You created stillness, night and day, reason and feelings,
    stars and sand,
seeming opposites of all sorts,
Yet you remained the same.

Then you stepped into your creation.

(1989)

Comes a smile…

Comes a smile
mysterious and ridiculous
showing wisdom and clumsy
knowledgeable lack thereof.

Comes a soft moment
when even the jaw indicates
hopeful wistfulness —
hope cannot be hid forever
neither from oneself
nor from the rest of the world.

Comes a giving,
a conceding, a joy,
and a loss of oneself
and the giving over of the "other"

who is free
whose belonging does not depend on,
yet already resides within me.

(1989)

At the Bank

for Alexandre

Academics who have worked in banks are not so uncommon.
I know several. But none I know would necessarily recommend it.
And (but you know this already), T.S. Eliot worked in a bank for
a long time, before changing his day-job to editor at Faber's.
I was thinking of Eliot in 1984 when the bank manager had a
birthday (that summer I had read *Four Quartets* for the first time)
so when the colleagues ordered him a stripper, I declined—
and purchased him a copy of *Four Quartets* instead.
He unwrapped the gift, as I sat across from his desk and
told him why: Eliot, poet, was a banker too.
He thanked me for it. (All howlers intended).
Actually, he seemed touched.
And when the stripper came, I was glad
I had done it. That was all all so tacky —
watching her strip at an office party with champagne
but someone there later slipped me
tickets to the Chicago Symphony Orchestra
and the other person who did not participate
in paying the stripper was the
earnest Muslim man I reported to
who was a good and fair supervisor. I learned an invaluable skill:
telexing and receiving L.O.C. from Jeddah, Riyadh, and Dubai
while viewing Lake Michigan from the 26th floor

because we were in a skyscraper (of course)
and we organized the occasional office lunch in Little Italy
where everyone's high heels looked even more chic
than when we were punching numbers—
using numeric keypads for data-entry
so I can hardly regret
having worked for four months at a French Bank.
It was my first full-time job after
graduation, and it taught me
to go back to school.

(2021)

American Nursery Rhymes and Other Poems

Live in the blessing,
not the trauma.
Live in the blessing.

Ellen Amster

I.

Georgy Porgie puddin and pie
KKKissed the whites and made them cry
When the blacks came out to play
Georgy Porgie blew em away.

II.

10 little 9 little 8 little Indians
7 little 6 little 5 little Indians
4 little 3 little 2 little Indians
No little Indian boys.

ooooooooooo

NORMANDY (1944 and 2004)

A place in France
where your great great uncle went
and where your aunt teaches
to (almost) pay her rent.

CLONE ME A DOLLY (1996)
Put your right egg in and your left egg out
And if it's all together shake it all about
Do the hokey pokey
Three in a hundred work
That's what it's all about

LATE CAPITALISM
Keep your heads empty and your stomachs full
Why don't they tell us that at school?

RACS
RACS is backwards for CARS
You were in the motor city
Which used to be mighty pretty
Until a highway ran through it.

THE KOREAN WAR
Uncle Jess was not a bore
So our Dad said
He fought the Korean War
And did not come back dead.

SMART BOMBS (1991)
Did you know that bombs could be smart?
My sister's smart, my momma's smart
But bombs? Now there's a fopping lie.
I'd rather hear my brothers fart.

EXPANSIONISM
Shirley Chisolm was not your usual "ism"
or your usual anything for that matter
wonder what she would have said about "rough riders"
maybe: expand your minds rather than your territories.

BAR CODES (1970)

Zip right through the checkout line
with the new zippy price codes
Be the first one on your block
to get priceless groceries.

JUNK MAIL ON CREDIT

The flyers they come
The people they go
To the shop to the store
And buy all the more.

WATCH OUT FOR POETS

Womanizer rhymes with poetizer :
wounds   from a long, wet   bough.

GET YOUR KISSES WHERE YOU CAN

Un baiser à Taizé
vaut deux à Montreux.

WEARING THEIR TANS LIKE TROPHIES

Wearing their tans like trophies
They come back
from the mountains
from the sea
and can only think to ask

Once Upon A Time

Once Upon A Time.
A poetress was
stricken by poetolatry
for a poetling.
His royal poetship
poetized, seeking her opinion
to see if poetly.
Poetasting
her response
resulting in poetomachia.
Poetaz, poetress went poetless.

Twice, Upon A Once.
When only poetette, Poetaz,
in poetese proposed poethood
to a poetician.
The poeticism caused him
to poeticule his way right out of
poetdom.
Poetito, bella ciao.

Horse and Buggy, A Variation

The curtains were drawn and Emma
clung to Léon like a wet sponge
And the carriage did not stop...

A little white powder
Gulped in haste, like sugar to a diabetic
And home to dodge questions
and field furniture possessors

And then a corpse drooling black liquid
and locks of black hair —
But Homais won the Croix d'Honneur.

If

If my hand were to
brush against your breast
so lightly
that you could not tell
if it were me
or the wind

If the palm of my hand rested
so warmly
on your cheek
that you could not tell
if it were me
or the noonday sun

If my breath approached

your ear in a whisper of leaves

signaling a rush of joy

Could you be so present to me

that

your presence

will always remain?

I discover I don't like everything you say

But I love

the way you say it.

Le Stage

À Camille Toutée

De samedi à samedi dans une maison avec piscine
sur un rond-point dans les Cévennes, toutes
directions à notre portée. Une de cinquante-quatre ans
jusqu'à celle de quatre-vingts, nous voilà autour
de toi Camille, et non sans des membres de ta famille…

Nous sommes là pour peindre, de l'eau et de la couleur
Et ton avis et ta main, et ton camion… et ton chien…
Une jolie ronde de danse qui sera une arabesque à douze
à l'accordéon de Jacques, après la bonne cuisine de Josette,
suivant la souriante Gisèle, nous sommes tous parés pour la fête.

Geneviève fait les comptes,
après avoir compté tous les enfants
de tous les villages qu'elle a peints…
et Anne trace des lignes si droites :
admirable travail, toute minutieux,
comme aussi les tableaux de Dominique.
Quant à Sylvie, on passe chez les Nabis
et les Fauves, favorables aux mauves.
Pour Rebecca ce sera tout en bleus subtils.
Martine, toute discrète, consolide les détails.

Et Camille, tes commentaires sont constructifs, constructeurs,
et ta main est sûre,
si bien que Florence ne la résiste pas,
et mon tableau réussit grâce aussi à toi.

Mais négligeons rien au rôle de Pépite
dans cette affaire, car elle sait bien détendre l'atmosphère,
par exemple quand Josette ose prendre telle pose
ou quand Jean-Pascal va en cousant.
Ce stage fut réussi, et non seulement amusant.

Raw War

R A W	W A R	R A W	W A R
A A	A A	A A	A A
W A R	R A W	W A R	R A W

Why don't the journalists mention the pollution caused by war?

No greenhouse gases caused by blowing up tanks?

Already 14,5 degrees as average temperature in 2022 —

We don't need another fire

bomb
drone
tank
trench
death
war

What on earth is Putin thinking, after a century of polluting—
nature—killing—war?

Why annex a country while the planet is burning?

And how many Ukrainians does OTAN think should be killed to win against Putin?

R A W	W A R	R A W	W A R
A A	A A	A A	A A
W A R	R A W	W A R	R A W

SPLAT !

Haïkus de Saint Jean

~ ~ ~ ~ ~ ~ ~

On ne peut qu'embrasser cette croix
sur la tête, ou sur la poitrine —
s'y blottir, comme l'apôtre Jean
dans le présent de cette présence —
Amour infini et éternel

~ ~ ~ ~ ~ ~ ~

1
Pas d'étoiles sans
lui : et la Lumière luit
dans les ténèbres.

Le Verbe s'est fait
chair et a campé parmi
nous — Ah? à suivre !

2
Marie était là :
« De l'eau fait du vin, mon fils,
pour eux, s'il te plaît. »

« Le meilleur des vins! »
Jésus fête la Pâque
À Jérusalem.

3
Naître de nouveau,
rentrer au Royaume par
un vent de l'Esprit.

Au fils de l'homme
croire, et tes œuvres par
lui seront en Dieu.

« L'ami de l'époux
est joyeux de décroître. »
(Jean-le-Baptiste)

4
En Samarie, la
la femme à la source l'entend
« Sois une source… »

Les disciples sont
étonnés de voir qu'il parle
avec celle-là.

5
« Lève-toi, marche ! »
dit Jésus, or c'est shabbat :
il n'est pas permis

de porter son lit.
Il s'en défend, ainsi Dieu
agit tous les jours :

Il est à l'œuvre.
Savoir : Jésus est Amour.
Son jugement est juste.

6
Alors devant la
foule, Jésus prit les pains,
il rendit grâce

et aux convives
il distribua poissons
et pains pour leur faim

« Rien ne se perd, oui,
rassemblez ce qui reste. »
Et le lendemain

Il dit: « Je suis pain
et vie: voyez et croyez !
Ne plus avoir soif ! »

7
C'était Sukkot et
Jésus monta au Temple
pour les enseigner :

« Si je parle de moi
je cherche ma propre gloire ;
si je parle de Lui

je suis véridique.
Celui qui m'a envoyé
est vraie Sagesse.

La loi de Moïse
vous ne la pratiquez pas.
Moi, je la connais.

Cessez de juger
selon l'apparence, mais
jugez justement. »

8
Adultère, la
femme apportée devant
lui, en plein délit…

« Toi, donc, que dis-tu? »
(Il écrivait sur le sol…)
« Sans pêché ? Jetez ! »

Ils partent tous, ne
reste que la femme et
lui, « va, ne pêche plus. »

« Du monde, je suis
La Lumière. Ne marche
pas aux ténèbres. »

« Mon témoignage
est valable parce que
je sais d'où je viens. »

« En vérité je
vous dis, avant qu'Abraham
existât, Je Suis. »

Ils veulent jeter
pierres contre blasphèmes
mais Jésus s'en va.

9
« Qui a péché, lui,
ou ses parents pour qu'il soit
aveugle comme ça ? »

Jésus répond, « Ni
lui ni eux, mais c'est que
Dieu sera connu.—

Du monde je suis
la lumière. » Et il crache
et fait une boue

pour les yeux, et dit :
« Va te laver : Siloé ! »
Et il voit claire.

« N'est-ce pas lui, le
mendiant ? » interrogent
les voisins. Que si.

L'homme raconte
partout son histoire mais
ses parents n'osent…

Jésus le revoit :
« Crois-tu au Fils de l'homme ? »
« Je te crois Seigneur. »

10
« Moi, je suis la voix
et la porte des brebis :
ils seront sauvés.

« Moi, je suis venu
pour qu'on ait la vie et
qu'elle surabonde ! »

« Je la dépose, ma vie
personne ne me l'enlève—
c'est ma liberté … »

À Jérusalem
il dit: « Vous ne croyez pas
vous n'écoutez pas.

Moi et le Père,
nous sommes un. Je donne
la vie éternelle. »

Pour le blasphème
la foule veut des pierres
pour le lapider.

Vas-tu en jeter ?
Le pasteur ou le brigand ?
quelle voix écouter ?

11
« Toi ici, il ne
serait pas mort mon frère. »
Marie dit pareille.

Jésus lui répond:
« Ton frère ressuscitera »
Et Jésus pleura.

À la grotte il
dit « Enlevez la pierre! »
« Non, il sent déjà! »

« Lazare, sors de
là! Viens dehors! » Et il sort
en bandelettes.

12
Les premiers Rameaux,
la veuille Jésus est chez
Marthe et Marie.

Marie prend du nard
et oint les pieds de Jésus.
Lazare est convive.

Parfumez les lieux !
Avec ses cheveux Marie
sèche les pieds du Christ.

Une foule vient
regarder Lazare vivant
et le Christ aussi.

Le lendemain ils
crient « Hosanna ! Béni soit
celui qui vient : Roi ! »

Jésus trouve un
âne et s'assit dessus,
conforme aux écrits.

« L'heure est venue, »
dit Jésus, « de glorifier
le Fils de l'homme. »

« Si le grain ne meurt
il demeure seul, mais s'il
meurt, il y a fruits. »

« Qui aime sa vie
la perd ; et qui haït sa
vie la sauve. »

« Si quelqu'un me sert,
qu'il me suive, et où je
suis, il sera là… »

13
Au cours du repas
avant la Pâques, Jésus
se lève de table

et lave les pieds des
disciples en essuyant
avec un linge.

Et il leur dit: « Vous
devez aussi vous laver
les pieds entre vous.

Ce que j'ai fait pour
vous, faites-le vous aussi.
Vous n'êtes pas plus

grand que le maître.
Vous serez heureux si vous
le faites ainsi.

Me recevoir, c'est
aussi recevoir celui
qui m'a envoyé. »

Le disciple que
Jésus aimait se trouvait
à côté de lui.

Il dit: « Seigneur, qui? »
À Judas Jésus donne
un morceau de pain.

Jésus lui dit: « Fais
vite ce que tu vas faire. »
Judas est sorti.

« Aimez-vous les uns
les autres, comme je vous
ai toujours aimés.

Ainsi vous serez
identifiés comme
mes vrais disciples. »

14
« Vous croyez en Dieu,
donc croyez aussi en moi.
Je vais chez mon Père.

Dans sa demeure,
il y a là votre lieu.
Je suis le chemin

la vérité et
la vie. Celui qui m'a vu
a vu le Père.

Le Paraclet vous
sera donné, l'Esprit saint,
la vérité vraie.

Si quelqu'un m'aime
il suit ma parole, et
mon Père l'aimera.

L'Esprit saint va vous
enseigner toutes choses.
Ma paix est pour vous. »

15
« Je suis la vraie
vigne et mon Père est
le bon vigneron.

Le sarment sans fruit,
il l'émonde. Demeurez en
moi, dans mon amour.

Si vous demeurez
en moi vous porterez du
fruit en abondance.

Nul n'a d'amour plus
grand que de donner sa vie
pour ceux qu'il aime. »

16
« On va vous exclure
des synagogues, et bien plus :
on vous tuera.

Mais l'Esprit connaît
le péché du monde et
il vous guidera.

Il va m'expliquer,
et me glorifier pour
vous, il restera.

Vous serez tristes
mais cela se changera,
d'un seul coup, en joie.

Je ne suis pas seul
le Père est avec moi et
vous aurez la paix. »

17
« Père l'heure est là,
glorifie ton fils pour qu'il
te glorifie.

Ceux-là croient que tu
m'as envoyé, et pour eux
je prie. Ils sont tiens.

Tout ce qui est à
moi est à toi et tout ce
qui est tien est mien.

Dans ton Nom garde-
les, pour qu'ils soient un comme
nous, et dans la joie.

Ils ne sont pas du
monde comme moi je ne
suis pas du monde.

Ne les sorte pas
du monde, mais préserve
leurs pas du Mauvais.

Je prie aussi pour
ceux qui croiront en moi par
eux : qu'ils soient tous un. »

18
Les disciples et
Jésus sont allés dans un
jardin près de l'eau.

Des gardes arrivent
aux lanternes et torches—
Judas avec eux.

« Vous m'avez trouvé, »
leur dit Jésus. « Laissez les
autres s'en aller. »

Pierre, avec un
glaive, frappe le servant
du grand prêtre et

Malchus avait mal
à l'oreille. Jésus, on
l'amène chez Anne.

Un peu plus tard on
demande trois fois à Pierre,
« n'es-tu pas des leurs ? »

On envoie Jésus
chez Caïphe, et Pierre
nia, coq chantant.

Pilate lui demande,
« Tu es le roi des juifs? »
« Pas de ce monde… »

« Quiconque est dans la
vérité entend ma voix. »
« Pour nous — Barabbas ! »

19
On fait flageller
Jésus avec couronne
d'épines et manteau

pourpre. Pilate
dit: « Voici votre roi ! » mais
eux: « Crucifie-le ! »

Et il est sorti,
portant sa croix au Crâne,
Golgotha, la mort…

« Le roi des Juifs »
Marqué en hébreu, latin,
Et grec. Devant tous.

Le bon larron dit,
« Jésus souviens-toi de moi
dans ton royaume. »

Habits partagés.
Les soldats tirent au sort
pour la tunique.

Près de la croix se
tiennent sa mère et sa
sœur et Magdala.

Jésus dit, « Femme,
voici ton fils. » et à Jean,
« Voici ta mère. »

Et Jean l'accueille
chez lui. Jésus dit, « J'ai soif. »
On lui offre du

vinaigre, il prend
et dit, « c'est achevé » et
rend son esprit, puis

Les soldats brisent
les jambes des deux autres,
mais pas de Jésus.

D'une lance un
soldat lui perce. Coulent
du sang et de l'eau.

Disciple caché,
Joseph d'Arimathie
Prend le corps du Christ.

Par Nicodème
du myrrhe et d'aloès —
vite l'embaumer,

le mettre dans un
tombeau neuf tout près, car c'est
la fête pascal.

20
La Magdala va
au tombeau tôt le matin
mais Il n'est pas là.

L'autre disciple
et Pierre courent aussi
les linges sont là

mais non pas Jésus.
Les disciples retournent
chez eux. Et Jean croit.

En pleurs, Marie de
Magdala se pencha
vers l'intérieur et

perçoit deux anges
vêtus de blanc au tombeau:
« Pourquoi tu pleures? »

« Je ne sais pas où
On l'a mis. » Se retournant,
Elle voit quelqu'un là.

Jésus dit: « Marie ! »
Elle lui répond: « Rabbouni ! »
« Ne me touche pas

mais va trouver les
autres, leur dire que je
monte vers mon Père. » ....

Les portes closes
les disciples se retrouvent
Jésus arrive :

« Paix à vous! » et il
leur montre ses mains et son
côté. « Paix à vous! »

« Comme le Père
m'a envoyé, moi aussi
je vous envoie. »

« Recevez l'Esprit
Saint. À qui vous remettrez
les péchés, ils sont

remis. » Huit jours plus
tard ils étaient là avec
Thomas. « Paix à vous, »

dit Jésus, « Thomas,
porte ton doigt ici : sur mes
mains. Avance ta

main dans mon côté,
ne sois plus incrédule! »
« Seigneur et mon Dieu! »

« Parce que tu me
vois, tu crois. Heureux ceux qui
vont croire sans voir. »

21
Simon Pierre dans
la barque. Un homme dit
« Le filet à droite! »

Tellement plein de
poissons, ils n'avaient plus la
force de tirer.

Jean dit à Pierre
« C'est le Seigneur! » À ces mots,
Il se jette dans l'eau

rejoindre Jésus
devant un feu de braise,
aux poissons et pains.

« Venez déjeuner, »
il prend le pain et donne
du poisson, et dit :

« Simon, m'aimes-tu ? »
Par trois fois cette question.
« Donne à mes brebis ! »

(2021-2022)

Boomer

For those preparing
to be teachers

They will keep you from getting older
their eyes and energy will uphold yours
and keep your brain supple and then
one day students will inform you
about how old you really are
and sometimes they'll say strange things:
"Thank you for showing me I might be able
to teach even though I'm on the spectrum,"
(strongly implying your own spectrum
score has been showing).

In a few of those mandatory classes
where uninterested ones were vengeful and
boldly dominated the receptive majority
they might call you a boomer — or worse —
say it's YOUR FAULT the climate changed
(well, yes, but not *only* mine —).

Or they tell you no other third-year
university language teacher ever required
them to buy books (!!) and then your highly
visible response could be to
age more than a decade in three seconds.

Of course they do not know about
degraded teaching conditions during
the past twenty years of constant
so-called 'university reforms' or
how some colleagues keep the best
groups and subjects for themselves forever
despite their lack of research and publishing
(entitlement being the modus operandi)
or how class sizes have been doubled
and extra teaching hours imposed
or about the grin-and-bear-it mentality
as the humanities get still less funding each year
—and then covid distance-teaching
and digital homework to grade—and
they have no idea what grading 1,000 essay
papers in a year is like. How could they?

Even so, sometimes their opening eyes
make you dance inside.

Multiple Choices

In Paris the war in Ukraine makes
shopping shocking and crunches the climate
and we must always cook ourselves
for restaurants are outside our
student/senior budgets

(pick one or both)

Yet we still count the days we strike,
and the years until we retire,
and style ourselves, for Art
who is a requiring Courtesan.

We visit the exhibit and we squirm
and then go home to
maybe DIY some Trash Art
while we watch TV. And you?

Chicago Picasso
is a Trojan Horse
with all of the warriors gone home to
join the Black Arts movement
or play a game of chess

(pick one or both)

The war that traumatized you the most was
(check all that apply)

Vietnam / Europe from 1914 to 1918 / Ukraine 2022- /
World War 2 / Iraq 1991 / Cambodia / Rwanda 1994 /
the Spanish Civil War / the War of 1812 /
the Second Italo-Ethiopia War 1935-1936 / January 6, 2021 /
the Pinochet Coup 1973 / the coup in Myanmar 2021 /
the war on drugs / Laos 1959-1975 / Iraq 2003 /
Afghanistan 2001-2021 / the Spanish-American War /
Pontiac's War / the Battle of Vinland / the American Civil War /
Queen Anne's War / the South Sudanese Civil War /
the Six-Day War 1967 / the Trojan War / add your war(s) here):

Which war was it that killed the climate?
If you read Sun Tzu
should you believe him?
Lao Tzu makes better reading...
The best art of war is
P E A C E

(2023)

Novembre 1996

Berlin. Visite du Mémorial de la Résistance
le filme de von Haeften devant Freisler
et Plötzensee, son lieu de mort
émue

Le mois précédant Geoffrey Hill
a récité son Bonhoeffer et laissé
une grosse tâche d'encre dans un livre
appartenant à Lesley

émue
sans taches de sang visibles
ma mère a quitté ce monde
juin 1996

Résistant à mon deuil
je viens de le retrouver

This Morning, the Sun

This morning the sun

like an apple in the sky

made me think of you

i.m. Mathilde Panoff (1964-2002)

Notes

My Momma I asked

The title makes a kind of response to Langston Hughes's *Ask Your Mama: 12 moods for Jazz* (1961).

Pep Talking the Alphabet

(Letter U) "Every Man a King!" was a political slogan used by Huey P. Long (1893-1935), and then a song written by Long and C. Carazo in 1935. Father Charles E. Coughlin (1891-1979) supported Long's presidential campaign. Coughlin became notoriously anti-Semitic, and his national radio program, broadcast from the National Shrine of the Little Flower Catholic Church in Royal Oak, Michigan, was criticized for pro-nazi content after he spoke positively about Kristallnacht in 1938.

Quatorze, ou bien plus

Les Franciscains inventent les stations de la croix au XIVe siècle pour aider les gens à apprendre l'histoire de la crucifixion du Christ.

Les sept dernières paroles du Christ sont tirées des textes des quatre évangiles, aucun évangile ne contient tous les sept.

Aujourd'hui, c'est surtout dans des églises catholiques que l'on voit les stations. Parfois visiter un lieu peut amener une réflexion approfondie. Nous recommandons particulièrement les stations de la croix que l'on trouve à la Maison de Saint Yves à Saint Brieuc ainsi que les sept dernières paroles du Christ que l'on trouve gravées dans les murs à la chapelle Notre-Dame de la Sagesse, Paris XIII.

I. Voir Matthieu 26.29.

II. Baudelaire, « Enivrez-vous » dans *Le Spleen de Paris*, XXXIII.

III. Voir Jean 11.35 et Psaume 144.12.

IV. Il existe une belle statue en émail, *Notre Dame de la Pleine Lumière*, de Léa Sham's et Alain Duban, à la Cathédrale Saint Étienne de Limoges.
VI. Michel de Montaigne, « De l'Amitié ».
VII. Psaume 94.6. « La Prière, » Poème de Francis Jammes, chanté par Georges Brassens.
VIII. André Gide, dans *Ainsi soit-il ou Les jeux sont faits*, 1952.
IX. Extrait de Psaume 101.6.
X. T.S. Eliot, *Les Quartre Quartros*, traduit de l'anglais par Claude Vigée (1992). T.S. Eliot, *Meurtre dans la Cathédrale*, traduit de l'anglais par Henri Fluchère (1943). George Herbert, « The Altar » dans *The Temple* (1633). Amos Oz, *Jésus et Judas*, traduit de l'anglais par Sylvie Cohen, Préface de Delphine Horvilleur, (Grasset, 2021). Martin Buber, *Ich un Du* /*Je et Tu* (1923).
XI. Extraits de Psaume 88.19 et de l'épître de Saint-Jacques 2.17.
XII. Les sept dernières paroles, à peu près telles qu'à Notre Dame de la Sagesse.
XIV. Dans tous les évangiles, ce sont des femmes (dont Marie-Madeleine) qui découvrent le tombeau vide.
XV. Luc 24.11, 22-24, 45.

Pantheon

V. L'Experte

Anne Mounic's review *Temporel* also finely illustrates her "pinball" talents. http://www.temporel.fr

VII. The People's Prof

During his lifetime and for several centuries, D'Alembert was known as D'Alembert. When Theodore Besterman invented the little 'd' and wrote "d'Alembert," John N. Pappas felt an obligation to strongly contest the change.

Yours

The first line is from Charles le Quintrec in "Licorne" from *La marche des arbres* (1970).

Contents

Imprimé en France
Achevé d'imprimer en novembre 2023
Dépôt légal : juillet 2023

Pour

Le Lys Bleu Éditions
40, rue du Louvre
75001 Paris